THE
DROITWICH
DECEIVERS

A captivating Victorian historical murder mystery

KERRY TOMBS

Inspector Ravenscroft Detective Mysteries Book 5

JOFFE
BOOKS

Revised edition 2020
Joffe Books, London
www.joffebooks.com

First published in Great Britain 2012

**Join our mailing list and become one of 1,000s of
readers enjoying free Kindle crime thriller, detective,
mystery, and romance books and new releases.
Receive your first bargain book this month!**

www.joffebooks.com

We love to hear from our readers! Please email any
feedback you have to: feedback@joffebooks.com

ISBN 978-1-78931-599-8

*For Joan — with love, for all her help
and encouragement over the years*

PROLOGUE

DROITWICH RAILWAY STATION, NOVEMBER, 1889

She stood on the cold, empty platform, holding the child of her joy and sin close to her shaking body, watching the train disappearing from view, through wet sorrowful eyes, and wondering how the pattern of her life had bought her to this unwelcoming place.

Drawing the shawl ever closer round the baby to protect the infant from the bitter wind, she began to walk quickly towards the waiting-room at the end of the platform, and pushed open the creaking door.

Relieved to discover that the room was empty of passengers, she sought the end of the old wooden bench near the grate which contained the burnt out remains of yesterday's fire, and placed the brown parcel on the seat beside her, before looking down into the face of her sleeping child — the child she had never thought possible, the child who had arrived so unexpectedly, the child who had been scorned by others, and who now lay peacefully in her arms.

Presently she turned her attention to the large clock which adorned one of the white washed-walls of the room, and for the next few minutes anxiously watched as the large hand moved on steadily. She wished with all her heart that she could halt its progress, but knew that now the decision had been made she could do little to alter that which had been set in motion.

As the hand reached the end of the hour, she grew restless and concerned. She had half expected the couple to meet her upon her arrival, then, once the train had arrived and departed, depositing and collecting no one, she had told herself that perhaps she had failed to comprehend the instructions within the letter: that the hour had been incorrect, or that she had mistaken the day. Now as the hand crept forwards into its next circle of time, she resolved to leave at the completed quarter, to give up her resolution and return once more to the scene of her disgrace.

Suddenly the door opened and a short, grey-haired woman, wearing a black bonnet and long coat stood on the threshold. 'You must be Alice?' she said smiling.

She had expected someone different, had assumed that the woman would be younger, and that her husband would be with her. 'Yes,' was all the young woman could reply.

'I am sorry I was delayed, my dear.'

'I thought your husband—'

'Detained on business in the city.'

She turned away from the new arrival and looked down at her baby.

'And is this your child?' asked the woman in a soft almost musical tone of voice, and smiled again as she seated herself beside her. 'What is her name, my dear?'

'Lily,' she answered in a voice that seemed like a distant forced whisper to its owner.

'Lily. What a pretty name! You would not object if we added Ann to her name, in memory of my late daughter, Clarisa Ann. There is hardly a day goes by when we do not think of her, the poor child. My husband and I would so like that, if we could call her Lily Ann,' said the woman sniffing, and bringing a handkerchief quickly to her eyes.

'Lily. That is her name,' Alice replied protectively drawing the child towards her.

'Of course my dear. I understand. May I hold the child?'

Alice looked into the woman's face unsure whether she would find kindness there amidst the well-worn features and tired eyes.

'May I?' repeated the woman, in a firmer tone of voice.

'I should want to know that she be taken well care of.'

'And so she shall, my dear,' replied the other reassuringly. 'As I said in my letter, my husband and I are so distraught by our loss. We only require some companionship in our old age. That is all we seek. We know that our lovely, sweet innocent daughter can never be given back to us, but the good Lord has sent you to us, in our hour of need. God be praised! Your child — Lily Ann — will want for nothing, I can assure you. My husband is an important man in the city and we live in a pretty, neat little house in Cheltenham, with two servants to attend to our every need.'

'Two servants?' she looked up, her eyes widening at the thought.

'Why yes. Mr Huddlestone would not have it any other way. We have all the comforts of a good Christian life. Upon my return today, I will hire a nurse to care for Lily Ann, and when she is older I will engage a private tutor to teach her to read and write and instruct her in the best of manners.'

'A tutor!' Alice exclaimed, almost unable to accept what she was being told by this strange woman.

'Your child will want for nothing when she is with us. You can rest assured that we will bring her up as if she were our own.'

'You are so very kind.'

'No, it is you who is kind, my dear. Why I said to Mr Huddlestone only yesterday that if we could bring a little Christian happiness into this ungrateful, sinful world, then our lives would not have been in vain. I believe that we have all been placed on this earth to fulfil God's purpose. May I?' smiled the woman reaching out to receive the child. 'Why, what lovely features she has. She is not unlike our dear Clarisa Ann in that respect.'

'Please let me have her back,' Alice pleaded, suddenly realizing that she had given away that which she valued above all other. 'Give me back my daughter!'

'Now then my dear, don't you go fretting and upsetting yourself. That will do neither you nor the baby any good. We mean her no harm, you know that.'

'But she is my daughter!'

'And what can you do for her, my dear, a poor servant girl like you? You will be fortunate indeed to find another position in your circumstances. No one wants an unmarried mother with a young child, these days. People have to be so careful; they cannot afford the disgrace. There is always the workhouse — but what start in life is that for the child? Such cold, unfeeling places. She would be fortunate indeed to survive the first year. I suppose the father does not want to do anything for you both? No, I thought not. They never do,' reprimanded the woman, shaking her head from side to side.

'No,' was all she could reply, and as she turned away tears again began to come to her eyes.

'You know that little Lily Ann will be better cared for with me and my husband. We can give her so much. But of course if you would rather bring up the child yourself?'

'No. I cannot.'

'You are doing the correct thing, my dear. The good Lord will look down upon you in future years and will bless you for your charity in giving Lily Ann this opportunity to better herself. You could not deny her that, my dear, could you?'

'No,' she sobbed.

'Good, then that is all decided upon. I think I hear my train drawing into the station,' announced the woman rising suddenly her the seat, whilst cradling the child in her arms. 'Now my dear, I don't like to mention it, but there is the question of a certain . . .' her voice trailed away.

'I'm sorry,' said the young mother reaching into her pocket, from which she withdrew a crumpled envelope.

'Just to cover our initial expenses, as agreed. Five pounds, my dear?'

'It is all I have,' Alice replied looking up into the woman's eyes as she passed over the envelope.

'You must look upon it as investment for your baby, my dear. Believe me I would not ask for anything, but Mr Huddlestone is quite particular in these matters,' said the woman adopting a firmer tone as she pushed the envelope into her coat pocket. 'And that must be the parcel?'

She said nothing as the woman reached out for the dirty brown package.

'A few things for the baby, no doubt as we suggested — just until we can purchase some new garments for Lily Ann, you understand. Now my dear, I do believe my train has arrived.'

'Please no!' she called out, quickly rising from the seat.

'Now then my dear, it is best if you stay here. It won't do the child any good if she wakes up now and sees you crying like that, it will only cause her more distress, and we don't want that do we?'

'No, I suppose not.'

'You just sit there for a few minutes. You know it is the right thing.'

'Can I see her?' she pleaded. 'Can I come and see her sometimes?'

'Of course you can, my dear. I believe you have my address. We reside at Number 22, Suffolk Square, Cheltenham. Do you know the town?'

'I have never visited there.'

'Suffolk Square is in the most fashionable part of Cheltenham, near Montpellier. Mr Huddlestone would not wish to associate himself with any less desirable quarter of the town, I can assure you. You would be most welcome to call upon us, shall we say in about six months?'

'That seems so long time,' she said through her tears.

'I think it would be unsettling for the child if you were to come sooner. We must allow the infant to become familiar with her new life. As a mother I am sure you understand that. Now we must go, before the train departs without us. It would never do if we were late returning. Mr Huddlestone would be so worried.'

'Please, may I look at my child one more—' she pleaded, but before she could complete her request, the woman had stepped out onto the platform, closing the door quickly behind her.

'No. No!' Alice cried out, throwing herself down on the bench, and covering her face with her hands as her body shook uncontrollably.

Through her tears she became aware of a whistle being blown and then the sound of the train commencing its slow exit from the station. 'Oh no!' she exclaimed, rushing towards the door.

'I'm afraid you've missed the 3.30, miss,' said the large, red-faced railway porter entering the room and blocking her way. 'Next train won't be for another two hours. Are you all right, miss?'

'The train. You have to stop the train,' she said pushing past the man and running out onto the platform.

'I can't do that, miss. Once the train has begun its journey it is too late,' replied the man following on behind. 'If you don't mind my saying so, you don't look very well, miss. Why don't you sit down for a minute, while I calls you a cab.'

But she did not hear his words, for as the smoke cleared from the station and the train disappeared from view down the track, the awful realization of what had just taken place suddenly swept over her and, covering her wet face with her trembling hands, she sank to her knees in despair.

CHAPTER ONE

LEDBURY, APRIL, 1890

'Samuel.'

'Yes, my dear,' replied the detective without looking up from his writing.

'Are you particularly busy at the moment?' asked Lucy.

'Just completing my monthly report, that is all.'

'And does your report contain anything of startling importance?'

'If you call the arrest of yet another of the Leewood clan for attempting to break into the town office buildings, and the rounding up of those two vagrants in the market place last week, major crimes, then yes, I suppose my report must be of the greatest importance to the police authorities,' grumbled Ravenscroft, throwing down his pen in annoyance.

'I am so sorry—' began Lucy.

'No, it is I who must apologize. You find me in a bad humour this evening. You must excuse me. It is just that life has been so dull and uneventful of late. Since that business in Tewkesbury last year there has been nothing to interest me at all. Not a decent robbery for months! No attempted murders! No major disturbances! I do not know what the world is coming to. I might as well not be here,' continued Ravenscroft in the same gloomy vein.

'There was that rather vicious argument outside the Feathers last month,' offered Lucy.

'Just two Irish navies who were celebrating St. Patrick's day. They soon sobered up after a night in the cells.'

'And don't forget that runaway horse which galloped all along the Homend, and who then threatened to turn over all the market stalls.'

'Tom soon brought it under control.'

'And then there was that one-eyed poacher who said he would burn down the church if the vicar ever—'

'Yes, yes, I know,' protested an irritated Ravenscroft.

'Perhaps it is your presence here that has led to the reduction in crime in Ledbury? I am sure any suspicious person, intent on criminal activity in this town, upon learning of your presence here, would quickly take himself off to Hereford or Worcester, or some other such place, to commit his unlawful outrage there.'

'Stop teasing me,' laughed Ravenscroft getting up from the table and walking over to the empty chair set before the blazing fire.

'Yes, I suppose life must be very dull after all your years in Whitechapel. Do you not sometimes wish you were back there again?'

'Not for one second, my dear. I did my time in London; let others now try to bring law and order to that den of iniquity. Fortunately you saved me from all that. I am a bad fellow indeed to complain when I have such a wife and children to make me happy. I suppose I only have one regret in leaving there.'

'Oh, and what might that be?' asked Lucy placing her book on the small side-table near her chair.

'I only wish I had been there when that Jack the Ripper character was about his work.'

'Oh Samuel, you surely don't think that you could have bought him to book, when everyone else failed?'

'I would have had a jolly good try. Every criminal makes a mistake, that leads to his arrest, sooner or later. It is all just a matter of time,' said Ravenscroft warming his hands before the fire.

'Well, no one caught the "Ripper".'

'No, I suppose they did not. I often wonder what happened to the fellow? Perhaps he just went off somewhere else and died — fell into a lake and drowned, slipped off the edge of a cliff, or got run over by a train, or something like that. Perhaps he is just biding his time, waiting to commit some further atrocity. Who knows? Anyway I am tired of all that. That's all in the past. What have you been reading my dear?'

'*The Strange Case of Dr Jekyll and Mr Hyde* by Robert Louis Stevenson,' replied Lucy.

'Oh Stevenson. Didn't he write *Treasure Island?* "Yo-ho-ho, and a bottle of rum"; "pieces of eight" and all that?'

'Yes, he did.'

'So what is so strange about this Jekyll and Hyde?' asked Ravenscroft affecting a mild interest.

'Well, they are both the same person.'

'Both the same person?'

'Yes. Doctor Jekyll is a kind, considerate man, a bit like you Samuel, but then he makes up this strange potion which he drinks and then he becomes this horrible man called Mr Hyde, who of course is nothing at all like you Samuel, even when you are in one of your bad moods.'

'I don't have bad moods,' protested Ravenscroft. 'I admit I get a little unsettled at times, usually when I am bored. Nothing a good crime waiting to be solved would not cure. Anyway no more of that. Tell me more about your book. I'm intrigued.'

'Well there isn't much more to say really, just that each time Dr Jekyll takes the potion he becomes more and more horrible and commits all kinds of terrible things.'

'Interesting.'

'I suppose the author is trying to say that we all have two sides to our character; one half of us is good, whilst the other is, well, bad.'

'I can see what he is getting at. I have certainly known men, and women, who have appeared quite respectable on the outside, who nevertheless concealed the most appalling criminal intentions. The good often masks the evil. You must tell me what happens to your Doctor Jekyll when you have finished your book. I trust he gets bought to account for his bad deeds.'

'Yes, perhaps he does,' replied Lucy turning away and looking into the fire.

Ravenscroft picked up the newspaper which lay on the table next to his arm chair, and turned over the front page.

'Samuel,' said Lucy breaking the silence, after some minutes had elapsed.

'I knew it,' said Ravenscroft lowering his paper and peering over the top of his spectacles. 'I knew you were just waiting to talk to me.'

'Well yes, but you were busy at the time.'

'You have my undivided attention now, my dear,' smiled Ravenscroft folding the newspaper and placing it on a side-table.

'Well, I have been thinking, quite seriously, of late, that perhaps we should all move elsewhere,' said Lucy leaning forwards to face her husband.

'Move elsewhere? I thought you liked Ledbury. We are all quite comfortable here, are we not?'

'Well yes, I suppose so, but that is the problem. Richard is nearly seven years of age, and little Arthur is now four months old and will soon be in need of his own room. I fear we are all running out of space.'

'Running out of space?' frowned Ravenscroft.

'It's all right for you of course, you are out most of the day, you don't notice these things, but when Susan is looking after Arthur in one room, and I am in here giving one of my students a piano lesson, poor Richard just has nowhere to play.'

'Nowhere to play?' interrupted Ravenscroft picking up his newspaper once more.

'Oh Samuel do listen — and stop repeating everything I say,' replied a frustrated Lucy.

'I'm sorry,' said Ravenscroft trying to sound sympathetic. 'I had not realized that things had become so difficult for you.'

'This is quite a small cottage, Samuel. When I first came here there was just Richard and I. Susan only came during the day. Then you arrived. Then Arthur was born — and then Susan had to move in full time to look after him, and then she had to have her own room to sleep in.'

'I see the problem. What do you suggest then, my dear?' said Ravenscroft throwing another log on the fire.

'Well perhaps we should look around for something a little larger, somewhere with an extra room, or two, and a garden would be quite nice, not a large garden, just a small lawn, where Richard and Arthur could play when the weather is fine.'

'I see,' nodded Ravenscroft.

'I know your remuneration is not large, but now that we have a bit put by, I think we could afford something else which would be more in keeping with your position.'

'And have you considered where we might move to? It may be difficult for us to leave Ledbury, unless another situation becomes available elsewhere. I know that both Worcester and Hereford are fully staffed at present. And then I don't know of any suitable properties in Ledbury.'

'There are plenty of properties available in Malvern,' suggested Lucy.

'Malvern?'

'I notice that you spend quite a deal of your time there, and Ledbury is still quite near for you to travel to everyday if you need to,' said Lucy becoming more animated as she rose from her chair and walked over to her husband. 'In fact, yesterday when I was in Malvern I went into one or two agents, and acquired the particulars of some rather interesting houses that are available to rent.'

'I see. You have been busy, my dear.'

'There is a particularly pleasant house near the common at the Wells, which has a delightful drawing room with a large window that overlooks the garden, which I know the children would enjoy. It has such a fine view. It also has an extra two bedrooms, one of which would form a very nice nursery for Arthur.'

'It would appear that you have already been to view the property.'

'I knew that you would not mind, Samuel. You must really come and see it, as soon as you are free. I know that once you have seen—'

Lucy's flow of words was suddenly interrupted by a loud knock on the front door.

'Whoever can that be at this time of night,' said Ravenscroft rising from his chair.

'It's Constable Crabb sir,' interrupted the maid entering the room closely followed by the young fresh-faced constable.

'Hello Tom, what brings you out here at such a late hour?' asked Ravenscroft.

'I'm sorry to intrude sir, Mrs Ravenscroft. I hope I am not disturbing you?'

'That's quite all right, Tom. We were not doing anything of great importance. You look quite out of breath,' said Ravenscroft.

Lucy let out a deep sigh as she regained her seat.

'Urgent message from Sir Charles Chilton. You are to come at once,' said Crabb brandishing a telegram in one hand.

'And who is Sir Charles Chilton?' asked Ravenscroft taking the telegram.

'Lives in Droitwich I believe. Something big in salt,' offered Crabb.

'Salt!' exclaimed Ravenscroft beginning to read the communication. 'IMPERATIVE YOU COME AT ONCE. MOST SERIOUS MATTER. CHILTON. SIR CHARLES. HILL COURT. DODDERHILL. DROITWICH. Is that all?'

'Just after that telegram was delivered another one arrived.'

'Oh, who from Tom?'

'Superintendent. Gives instructions that you are to go to Droitwich as soon as possible,' said Crabb taking out another telegram from the top pocket of his tunic and passing it over to his superior.

'I don't know why someone from Worcester can't go,' said Lucy. 'It is rather late in the evening to venture out.'

'Or even from Droitwich. We have got a police station at Droitwich, haven't we?' asked Ravenscroft.

'Don't know sir, but I would have thought so,' replied Crabb.

Ravenscroft opened the second telegram and read, 'RAVENSCROFT. GO TO SEE SIR CHARLES CHILTON AT DROITWICH IMMEDIATELY. HAS ASKED FOR YOU PERSONALLY. MOST IMPORTANT THAT YOU COMPLY.

'Well Tom, I suppose there is nothing else for it; we will have to go forth into the night air and take ourselves off to Droitwich.'

'I believe there is a train leaving from Ledbury in fifteen minutes which will take us there sir,' said Crabb.

'Then we should make all haste up the Homend. I'm sorry my dear, I am afraid we will have to continue this discussion another time. Why on earth they have asked for me instead of using the local man is beyond me? Please don't wait up for me. I don't know when we will return.'

'Go Samuel, go now, or you will miss your train. As you said, we can finish our conversation another time,' said Lucy. 'Now do take care.'

CHAPTER TWO

DROITWICH

'Well, Tom, what do we know about this Sir Charles Chilton?' asked Ravenscroft as the two men sat in the carriage of a train which had left the town of Ledbury some twenty minutes before. They were now drawing out of the station in Worcester. 'You said he had something to do with salt.'

'Yes sir. Droitwich is famous for its salt. They have been digging it up for centuries by all accounts. Quite a hive of activity. And all I know is that Sir Charles seems to own most of it,' replied Crabb.

'And how did you come by this information?' asked Ravenscroft staring out of the window at the receding oil lamps on the station platform.

'Local newspaper, sir. Some weeks ago, there was an article on the salt manufacture at Droitwich, and I thought I remembered that Sir Charles's name was mentioned more than once or twice.'

'I see. I must say that I am more than intrigued as to why we have been summoned, and at such a late hour as well. I would have thought they would have requested assistance from the local station. The telegram said it was a most serious matter. Well we shall see.'

A few minutes later the train pulled into Droitwich station and the two men alighted from their carriage.

'Take us to Hill Court at Dodderhill, my man,' instructed Ravenscroft addressing the driver of the lone cab that was waiting outside the dimly lit station.

'You must be Ravenscroft then,' remarked the cabman indicating that the two men should enter.

'It seems we are expected, Crabb,' said Ravenscroft. 'How long will it take us to get there?'

'Five to ten minutes sir,' replied the cabman.

Ravenscroft and Crabb sat back in their seats, as the man cracked his whip and the horse broke into a brisk trot.

'How did he know who we were?' asked Crabb.

'I suppose Sir Charles assumed that we would arrive by train, rather than making our own way by road at this time of night,' replied Ravenscroft.

'Can't quite see where we are going,' said Crabb staring out of the window as they passed along the darkened streets of the town.

Presently the cab made its way up a steep hill before turning sharply to its left.

'I think I can see the lights from the house,' said Ravenscroft leaning out of the window as their conveyance made its way up a long driveway.

'Looks as though it could be a residence of some importance,' suggested Crabb.

The vehicle swung abruptly to the left before coming to a rest in front of a fine Georgian building. An elderly, grey-haired servant holding a lantern came forwards to meet them. 'Good evening sir. Welcome to Hill Court. If you would care to enter, Sir Charles is waiting for you in the entrance hall,' said the man opening the cab for the two policemen.

Ravenscroft made his way through the large open doorway observing, in passing, the ornate pillars and cornice which together framed the entrance.

'Ah Ravenscroft, good of you to come,' announced the squat middle-aged man, whom Ravenscroft found himself facing; this character sported a large, ginger handlebar moustache and mutton chop whiskers, and was smoking a massive cigar, dressed in evening attire.

'I came as soon as I received your telegram, Sir Charles. This is Constable Crabb, my assistant,' replied Ravenscroft.

'This is my solicitor and associate Mr Brockway. Thought it best if he were here.'

Ravenscroft nodded in the direction of the tall, elderly, grey-haired man who stood nervously by Sir Charles's side.

'Oh Mr Ravenscroft, I am so glad you have come,' called out a woman's voice from within one of the nearby rooms.

'This is my wife Ravenscroft, Lady Chilton,' said Sir Charles, as the lady in question entered the hallway.

'How-do-you-do, Lady Chilton,' said Ravenscroft observing the look of anxiety in the new arrival's face.

'You must help us, Mr Ravenscroft. It is all so terrible! We do not know whom to turn to,' said the woman grasping hold of Ravenscroft's hand and staring vacantly into his eyes.

'Now my dear. You best leave this to Brockway and I to deal with', said Sir Charles taking hold of Ravenscroft's shoulder and steering him in the direction of the study.

'But . . . but I should so like . . . I think it important . . .' began the woman, her voice full of concern as her words trailed away.

'I will tell Inspector Ravenscroft all he needs to know. Best if you retire, Mary,' said Chilton in a firm raised voice. 'Ravenscroft, after you.'

Ravenscroft and Crabb entered the book-lined study. Chilton and Brockway followed after them, the former closing the door behind the party.

'You must excuse my wife, Ravenscroft, this affair has distressed her somewhat. Not good for her nerves. Sure you will understand. Well take a seat, man,' said Chilton indicating that Ravenscroft should take the large leather armchair that was positioned at the side of the marble fireplace.

'Thank you sir,' replied Ravenscroft accepting the seat. Chilton seated himself at the other side of the large oak desk which seemed to take centre stage in the room. Brockway took the other chair at the side of the desk. Crabb took up position by the closed door and took out his note book from the top pocket of his tunic.

'You're probably wondering what all this is about,' said Chilton pausing to take a pull on his cigar as he stared at the middle-aged, balding, bespectacled detective seated before him.

'You said it was a matter of great importance,' said Ravenscroft feeling slightly uncomfortable in his new surroundings, as he glanced at the old master paintings that hung between the bookcases on the walls of the study.

'And so it is, man; it is of the gravest concern. I'll come straight to the point. My daughter has been taken.'

'I see.'

'Taken this afternoon from underneath our very eyes! If I find out who is behind this, I'll have the man hung, drawn and quartered! You just can't go around taking other people's children.'

'You say your daughter has been taken,' said Ravenscroft leaning forwards in his chair. 'How old is your daughter Sir Charles?'

'My daughter, Mildred, is nine years old.'

'And where was she taken from?'

'In the churchyard at Dodderhill.'

'Did anyone witness her abduction?'

'Well no one actually saw her being taken, but taken she was. No doubt about it. What I want to know, is what you are going to do about it?' said Chilton taking another puff on his cigar, as he leaned forwards and peered at the detective through the drifting smoke.

'Perhaps if you could be a little more specific, sir,' suggested Ravenscroft sensing the impatience in his host's voice.

'My daughter was walking in Dodderhill churchyard this afternoon with her governess, Miss Petterson. They were on their way into town — there is a path that leads from the side entrance of the house into the churchyard, then descends into the town. Anyway, Ravenscroft, apparently Petterson went into the church for a minute or so, on some business or other, and when she returned Mildred had gone. Nowhere to be found.'

'I see. Perhaps your daughter ran off and hid somewhere? A game of hide and seek maybe?' suggested Ravenscroft.

'My daughter is not in the habit of running off and hiding!' snapped Chilton.

'Did the governess, Miss Petterson make a search of the churchyard?'

'Of course she did, man.'

'And what happened next?'

'She ran back here, raised the alarm, and then the servants ran back to the churchyard and made a more thorough search of the grounds, all to no avail. My daughter was nowhere to be seen.'

'Did Miss Petterson see anyone else in the churchyard at the time your daughter was taken?' asked Ravenscroft.

'No. I believe not.'

'You mentioned that there is a path that leads from the churchyard down into the town. Your daughter could have run off that way?'

'I've told you, Ravenscroft, that my daughter is not the kind of girl to run off on her own. Damn it man, it is clear as a pikestaff that she has been taken,' growled Chilton chewing on his cigar.

'After your servants searched the churchyard, what happened next?'

'What do you mean — what happened next?'

'Well, did you report the matter to the local constabulary for instance?' asked Ravenscroft looking up at Crabb for a moment to see that his constable was taking notes.

'No. I was not in the house at the time of my daughter's disappearance. I was visiting the works at Stoke Prior, on business you understand. One of the servants rode over there with the news. Of course I returned to the house as soon as possible. My wife and I then gave orders that the grounds, and then the house were to be searched from top to bottom. The servants found nothing. That was when I decided to send for you, Ravenscroft.'

'Forgive me sir, but why did you send for me? There is a perfectly good station in the town I believe, they could have dealt with this matter.'

'I sent a message first to your superior, whom I have met socially on a number of occasions. He recommended you. Said you were the best man to deal with this matter, and that you were not too busy at the moment. Now what I want to know, is what you are going to do about finding my daughter, Ravenscroft?'

'You said, Sir Charles, that you believe your daughter has been taken?' said Ravenscroft choosing to ignore the last remark.

'Well of course she has been taken, man,' replied Chilton irritably.

'Can you think of anyone who would have taken your daughter sir?'

'Plenty, man. Look here Ravenscroft, I'm an important local business man, as I am sure you know. Salt is my business. Most of the town is dependent on my endeavours. I inherited the business from my father. It wasn't much then, but over the years through damned hard work I've made a success of it. We have a tidy pile put by, for a rainy day, if you understand my meaning — and you don't get where I am today without treading on a few toes on the way,' said Chilton leaning back in his chair and brushing away the surrounding smoke with a brisk swat of his hand.

'But no particular name comes immediately to mind?'

'No. I'll have Brockway here draw up a list of those I've had dealings with recently, if you think that would be of assistance. You can do that, Brockway?'

'Of course sir,' replied the solicitor.

'Why do you think your daughter was taken sir?' asked Ravenscroft.

19

'Money! Someone has obviously taken her — and they want money, I have no doubt of it.'

'But you have received no communication as yet?'

'No. If I had, I would not be sitting here like this would I? Get my daughter back Ravenscroft. She is all my wife has in this world. I'll pay you well,' said Chilton stubbing out his cigar in an ashtray, before rising quickly from his seat.

'We will do our best, sir,' said Ravenscroft feeling compelled to stand likewise, and realizing that his host was anxious to draw their conversation to an end. 'However, I cannot accept any payment. That is against police regulations.'

'As you wish Ravenscroft, as you wish. Now, where do you want to start?'

'Perhaps I could have a word with Miss Petterson, the governess,' suggested Ravenscroft.

'Whatever for?' asked Chilton.

'She was the last person to see your daughter before her disappearance.'

'Yes I know, but I've told you what she said. Can't see what else she can tell you.'

'Nevertheless sir, I would like to hear the account of your daughter's disappearance from Miss Petterson in person, if I may,' requested Ravenscroft firmly.

'Very well then,' sighed Chilton opening the door and calling to one of the servants to fetch the governess.

'And if I could have that list Mr Brockway, as soon as possible, I would be obliged,' said Ravenscroft turning towards the solicitor.

'Of course sir,' replied Brockway forcing a brief smile.

'You have known Sir Charles long?' inquired Ravenscroft.

'For the past thirty years, or more. I was previously employed by his father, Sir Christopher.'

'Ah Ravenscroft, this is Miss Petterson,' said Chilton re-entering the room follow by a tall, thin-faced, plainly dressed woman.

'Miss Petterson,' said Ravenscroft shaking the newcomer's hand.

'Mr Ravenscroft. This is a terrible business,' said the governess.

'It is indeed, Miss Petterson. I wonder, Sir Charles, whether I might speak with Miss Petterson alone?'

'Well yes. I suppose so, if you think it will help.'

'I do not mind Sir Charles if you should wish to stay,' offered Miss Petterson throwing her employer an quick anxious glance.

'I would prefer it, if we talked alone,' insisted Ravenscroft smiling.

'Well we'll leave you to it. Come on, Brockway. Let me know if you want anything, Ravenscroft,' replied Chilton making his way towards the door.

'Thank you, Sir Charles. Miss Petterson, if you would care to take a seat. Crabb, bring the chair over if you will,' said Ravenscroft.

Chilton and Brockway left the room, closing the door behind them, as the governess accepted the seat.

'Miss Petterson, perhaps we could begin by your telling us what happened this afternoon,' began Ravenscroft resuming his seat in the leather armchair.

'Well, I went into the church and when I came out again Mildred had gone,' offered the governess speaking in a quiet, matter-of-fact voice.

'If you could tell us in more detail what occurred,' interrupted Ravenscroft.

'Yes, of course. I'm sorry. Mildred and I left the house just after three o'clock this afternoon. We walked through the churchyard. I went into the church. Mildred said she would be quite happy looking at the stones. She always enjoyed reading the old inscriptions. Then I came out of the church and found that Mildred was not there. I thought for a minute that she was playing a game, hiding behind one of the vaults or stones, so I called out and then I searched the churchyard. When I failed to find her, I ran back to the house, informed the servants, and we all then made another search of the church grounds, and then the house. It is terrible. I feel so responsible.'

'Tell me, Miss Petterson, did you often walk through the churchyard with your charge?' asked Ravenscroft.

'Yes, we would often walk into town that way, two or three times a week.'

'When you entered the churchyard today did you notice anything unusual?'

'Unusual?'

'Was there anyone else there?'

'No, no one else.'

'When you ran back to the house, how long was it before you returned to the churchyard with the servants?'

'About ten minutes I suppose.'

'So if Mildred had been hiding, she would have had time to make her way elsewhere?' suggested Ravenscroft.

'I do not think that would have been possible. I can assure you that I made a thorough search of the churchyard before I ran back to the house. Had she been hiding there I am sure I should have found her.'

'She could have slipped into the church when you weren't looking, miss,' said Crabb looking up from his notebook.

'The servants also made an extensive search of the church,' corrected the governess.

'And how long were you in the church, before you came out again, and found that Mildred was not there?' continued Ravenscroft.

'Not more than five minutes, I suppose, Mr Ravenscroft.'

'Can you think of any reason why Mildred was taken?'

'None.'

'Had you or Mildred spoken to any strangers on one of your recent walks through the churchyard?'

'No, I cannot recall meeting any strangers recently.'

'Could you provide us with a description of the clothes that your charge was wearing at the time of her disappearance? Crabb, write this down if you will,' instructed Ravenscroft.

'Mildred was wearing a light green dress, with brown shoes and coat, and also a grey bonnet,' replied the governess.

'Thank you, miss,' said Crabb.

'I wonder whether you have a photograph of Mildred?'

'Yes Inspector. There is one over there on the small side desk. Shall I get it for you?'

'I'd be obliged.'

The governess walked over to the table, picked up the photograph, and handed it to Ravenscroft before resuming her seat.

'Thank you, Miss Petterson,' said Ravenscroft looking down at the photograph of the young girl with the smiling face and long ringlets.

'That was taken about a year ago. The image is a particular favourite of Lady Chilton. Since then Mildred has had a different hair-style. The ringlets have been replaced by long straightened hair.'

'Would you mind if I retained the photograph? It may be helpful in our enquiries.'

'Yes, I am sure that Lady Chilton would not object.'

'Thank you, Miss Petterson. May I ask how long you have been Mildred's governess?' asked Ravenscroft.

'I have resided here for the past three years. Before that Mildred had been in the care of a nurse, but when she attained the age of six, Sir Charles and his wife thought it best to employ a governess.'

'And before that? Were you employed as a governess elsewhere?' asked Ravenscroft interested in knowing more of the governess's history.

'Yes. I was a governess with Lord and Lady Roberts of Warminster House. I looked after their son for five years.'

'And why did you leave that employment?'

'Charles, my charge became old enough to go to a boarding-school.'

'Thank you, Miss Petterson, I am obliged,' said Ravenscroft suddenly standing up. 'I know it is dark and late at night, but I would like to visit the churchyard. Would it be possible to obtain some lanterns, and then if you would accompany us, retracing your steps this afternoon, that would be most helpful.'

'Yes of course. I will see if I can get one of the servants to go with us,' replied the governess rising from her chair and walking over to the door.

'Oh, just one more question Miss Petterson — why did you go inside the church?' asked Ravenscroft smiling.

'Why did I go into the church?'

'Yes, Miss Petterson — why did you go inside the church?'

'I cannot remember. Oh . . . I . . . yes, I wanted to see what hymns had been selected for next Sunday's service.'

'Why was that?' asked a perplexed Ravenscroft.

'I like to see which hymns have been chosen, so that Mildred and I can go over the words together.'

'I find that rather strange, Miss Petterson.'

'I am sorry, Inspector, I am not making myself clear. Because we all attend church on a Sunday morning, and because Mildred has to join in the singing, I find it helps her if we can go through the words beforehand. That is why I went into the church, to see which hymns had been selected.'

'I see. Thank you, Miss Petterson.'

'I will go and ask the servants for some lanterns.'

'I would be obliged.'

* * *

A few minutes later Ravenscroft, Crabb and the governess accompanied by the servant who had first greeted their arrival, closed the front door of the house behind them.

'Now, Miss Petterson, if you would kindly retrace the route that you and Mildred took to the church today,' requested Ravenscroft.

'Yes. If you would care to follow me, gentlemen,' replied the governess leading the way down the path at the side of the building. 'This leads through the kitchen gardens to the side entrance.'

'I see that the door is bolted on the inside,' said Ravenscroft when the party arrived at the end of the garden. 'Was it locked this afternoon?'

'No, it is only bolted in the evening. As you can see it opens out at the end of the road and just over there is the gate that leads into the churchyard,' indicated Miss Petterson.

The group made their way through the gate and up the narrow path that ran towards the church; the servant took the lead, holding the lantern high so that all could see their way.

'Here is the church, gentlemen,' announced the governess presently, bringing the party to a halt.

'And is this where you left Mildred?' inquired Ravenscroft.

'Yes. I remember that she said she would like to read the stones, whilst I went inside,' replied Miss Petterson.

'Church appears to be locked, sir,' said Crabb after stepping into the porch and failing to turn the large metal handle on the outside of the door.

'I believe the vicar locks the door at night. There have been one or two night thefts in the area recently, Inspector,' said the servant.

'That is interesting, Mr. . . ?'

'Jukes sir,' replied the servant.

'Thank you Mr Jukes. So, Miss Petterson you went through the door into the church, leaving your charge here, and then you returned five minutes later to find that she had disappeared?' asked Ravenscroft addressing the governess.

'That is correct, Inspector.'

'Tell me, Miss Petterson, when you went into the church, did you leave the door open, or did you close the door behind you?'

'I cannot remember. I may have closed the door behind me, but I am not sure.'

'You see the reason I ask, is that if Miss Chilton had been taken against her will, she would in all probability have cried out in the ensuing struggle, in which case you would have heard the sounds and been alerted to her plight,' suggested Ravenscroft.

'I see. Yes I see. I suppose I must have closed the door behind me then, as I heard nothing.'

'Thank you, Miss Petterson, that is most helpful,' said Ravenscroft turning away. 'I am not sure that much can be gained by continuing our investigations here tonight. Perhaps you would be kind enough to conduct us all back to the house, Mr Jukes. Quiet all of you! What is that noise?'

'I can't hear anything sir,' said the servant.

'Listen. I'm sure — yes, there it is again — a low grumbling kind of sound,' said Ravenscroft.

'I see what you mean, sir. Sounds more like a laughing sound to me,' offered Crabb.

'You're right, Crabb. It sounds almost as though someone were laughing at us — a low, sarcastic, a mature voice I would think. Hold the lantern higher, Mr Jukes. Yes, over there. It's coming from behind that large vault at the edge of the churchyard. Come out whoever you are! Show yourself!' commanded Ravenscroft running towards the monument, closely followed by the others.

'He's gone!' exclaimed Crabb bringing the other lantern to bear on the stone.

'Over there, sir,' cried out Jukes. 'I saw something running out of the churchyard.'

'Where does this path lead?' asked Ravenscroft. 'Look, there is someone running lower down the slope. Quickly, Crabb, get after him. We will follow on behind.'

The constable raced down the path after the disappearing figure, as Ravenscroft and his two companions followed.

A few moments later, Ravenscroft found himself at the foot of the path.

'Gone sir. He was too quick for me,' said a breathless Crabb.

'Never mind Tom, you did your best, given the darkness and the unfamiliar terrain. Did you get a good look at him?'

'Afraid not sir, but one thing I am sure about. It cannot have been the girl. I would say the figure was a full grown man by the size of him. Seemed to be wearing an old cloak.'

'That's interesting. Tell me, Miss Petterson, you said earlier that this path would eventually take one into the town?'

'Yes, that is so,' replied the governess.

'Did anyone in the search party come down this way?'

'No. After searching the churchyard and inside the church, it was thought that perhaps Mildred had returned to the house, so we all turned our attention there.'

'I see. We appear to be quite close to the railway line, and if I am not mistaken that must be water over there,' said Ravenscroft pointing.

'That is the canal, sir,' offered the servant, 'And beyond that is the River Salwarpe.'

'So there is a possibility that if Miss Chilton came this way, she could have met with an accident, either on the railway line, or by falling into the water.'

'Oh no!' cried out the governess.

'Quickly Crabb — I think the lady is about to faint!'

CHAPTER THREE

DROITWICH

'Anything to report constable?' asked Ravenscroft.

'Nothing as yet sir. We have examined the railway track and can find nothing there, and the men have just started to drag the river,' replied the uniformed officer.

It was the following morning, and Ravenscroft and Crabb had just arrived on the misty banks of the River Salwarpe, where a reluctant sun was attempting to break through the overhead clouds.

'When you have finished here, I want the men to drag the canal for a few hundred yards in either direction.'

'As you wish, sir.'

'Where does the canal go?' inquired Ravenscroft.

'Further along that way to the salt works in the town. The barges then make their way along the canal in that direction for a few miles towards Hanbury,' replied the policeman pointing.

'And after Hanbury?'

'That is where the canal joins the Worcester to Birmingham Canal, sir.'

'I see. Thank you, my man. Please do not let us detain you,' said Ravenscroft walking away. 'This is a strange case, Tom. Young girl taken in broad daylight — snatched from under her governess's nose, and yet there has been no demand for money.'

'Strange indeed,' replied Crabb.

'Do you know what I find distinctively odd about all this? When the girl disappeared the servants apparently made a thorough search of the church and churchyard, and yet none was sent down here, to see whether the girl had made her way to the river or canal. Furthermore, why did they waste time sending for us, when they could have had the local constabulary making a search round here within minutes of the girl disappearing? In my experience, Tom, the first two or three hours are the most crucial in cases like this. By the time we arrived it was already dark and the trail had run cold.'

'I see what you mean, sir.'

'In fact I am not all that sure that Sir Charles Chilton was very concerned about the disappearance of his daughter; his wife seemed more distressed than he does.'

'Yes, I noticed that, sir.'

'And did you see how quickly he ushered us into the study, when we arrived last night, so that we could not engage his wife in conversation? He seemed quite anxious that we would not have words with her.'

'The man is a bit of a bully I would say.'

'Yes, I must say I did find him somewhat intimidating. I think Sir Charles Chilton is a man who is used to having his own way in this world. Not the kind of person to cross swords with.'

'That governess is a queer fish as well,' added Crabb. 'Fancy leaving her charge unattended like that. Asking for trouble if you ask me.'

'Quite. I agree it seems negligent on her part. She seemed very calm about the whole affair, however.'

'Except when she fainted.'

'Yes Tom, but do we believe what she is telling us? I don't really accept that story about her going into the church, to see which hymns had been selected for next Sunday's service. She only came up with that story when we pressed her. I suppose there is a remote possibility that she is telling us the truth, but if she did go into the church, it would surely have been natural for her to have left the door open, given that her charge was playing outside.'

'It seems a bit careless,' added Crabb.

'She said she thought the door was closed, and claims that she heard nothing from outside. If the girl had been overpowered surely she would have cried out, and Miss Petterson would have heard, even though the door was closed, I would have thought.'

'Girl could have been overpowered by some cloth held to the mouth that would have rendered her speechless?' suggested Crabb.

'You might be correct. Still I would like to know a lot more about our Miss Petterson.'

'The girl could have left on her own account?'

'In which case that would explain why there was no noise. I suppose she could have met someone she knew, and the two of them then left together, but at this stage all this is conjecture,' said Ravenscroft glancing upwards to the church, on the large rocky outcrop, with its view over the river and canal.

'Then there is that strange fellow in the churchyard,' added Crabb.

'Yes, I wonder what he was doing there at that time of night?'

'Could have been some kind of vagrant.'

'Perhaps. Anyway we need to try to find him.'

'What do we do next, sir?' asked Crabb.

'Well in the absence of any body at present, and the fact that we have no witnesses to the time she disappeared, we must assume that the girl has been abducted. I will go back to the house and interview the servants. In my experience it is the servants who know everything that takes place in these large country houses. I will also try and interview Lady Chilton. It will be interesting to see what she has to say.'

'And what would you like me to do, sir?'

'I would like to know more about the governess. Go to the telegraph office and see if you can send a message to this Lord and Lady Roberts of Warminster. Ask them why the governess left, and whether they can vouch for her character. We need to know whether she has been telling us the truth. I noticed that there is an inn near the bottom of the path that leads up to the churchyard — the Gardeners Arms, I believe. It might be worth your while making enquiries there in case they saw anything yesterday. Then I want you to ask around the town and find out all you can about Sir Charles Chilton. See what folk make of him. I will meet you back at the house,' instructed Ravenscroft beginning to make his way back up the path towards the churchyard.

* * *

'Good morning to you, Inspector,' said Brockway greeting Ravenscroft as he entered Hill Court.

'Good morning Mr Brockway. I trust that there is still no news regarding young Miss Chilton?' asked Ravenscroft closing the door behind him.

'Nothing at all,' replied the solicitor.

'I have some men searching the river and canal. Hopefully they will not find anything, but we are bound to begin there.'

'Of course. All of this has come as a great shock to Sir Charles and his wife. We must hope that this matter reaches a speedy, satisfactory conclusion.'

'Indeed.'

'I have that list you asked for, Inspector. These are all the people Sir Charles has done business with in the past few years,' said Brockway reaching into the top pocket of his coat.

'Thank you,' said Ravenscroft taking the sheet of paper and studying its contents. 'This is rather a long list of names.'

'Sir Charles has dealings with a great many people,' remarked the solicitor drily.

'And is there anyone on this list who has, shall we say, had a falling out with Sir Charles, and perhaps bares a grudge against him?' inquired Ravenscroft.

'There is no one that immediately springs to mind.'

'Oh, come now Mr Brockway, there must be someone on this list whom Sir Charles has had difficulties with recently?'

'Well I suppose there is someone. Mr Russell. Mr James Russell. You will see his name towards the bottom of the paper,' said Brockway reluctantly.

'And who is this Mr Russell?'

'He owns some land on the edge of the town, which he farms in a small way, a family concern I believe, inherited from his parents. You will find his property towards the end of Vines Lane.'

'Why did Sir Charles and this Mr Russell fall out?'

'Sir Charles wishes to purchase some of Mr Russell's land. Mr Russell refuses to sell. It is as simple as that.'

'And why does Sir Charles wish to purchase Mr Russell's land?' asked Ravenscroft with interest.

'We — Sir Charles believes there is an old salt pit on the land.'

'I see. And Sir Charles would wish to mine the salt deposits?'

'Sir Charles has made an offer, a very generous offer for the land, well above its agricultural value.'

'But Mr Russell does not wish to sell?'

'Quite.'

'Have any threats been made by this Mr Russell?'

'Oh dear no. It has not come to that. I will admit that some sharp words have been exchanged on both sides on the matter, but there has never been anything of that nature. In fact I am sure that Mr Russell cannot be behind all this. I only mentioned his name because I was pressed. Now if you will excuse me Inspector, I have to attend a business meeting at the Raven Hotel,' said Brockway after quickly consulting his pocket watch.

'Is Sir Charles available to speak to me this morning?' asked Ravenscroft.

'I am afraid Sir Charles has been called away on urgent business at nearby Stoke Prior.'

'When do you expect his return?'

'I am afraid I cannot say, Inspector.'

'Then may I speak with Lady Chilton.'

'Oh, I'm afraid that will not be possible.'

'Why?'

'Lady Chilton is not well today and is confined to her room: All this has proved a great strain for her, as I am sure you will appreciate.'

'Nevertheless I would like to speak with her. She may be able to provide us with valuable information,' said Ravenscroft determined not to be refused.

'As I said, Lady Chilton is indisposed. Now you simply must excuse me. I am late already. Good day to you sir,' said Brockway stepping quickly past Ravenscroft and out through the door.

Ravenscroft stood silently in the hall, contemplating the solicitor's answers. Why had Brockway refused him permission to speak with Lady Chilton? Surely it would have been in the family's interests for him to have interviewed the mother of the missing girl? She above all others, might well have been able to shed light on the mystery. Then there was the question of the list of names which Brockway had provided — so many names, and yet the solicitor had only been able to pick out the name of Russell, a local landowner, with whom Sir Charles had had a minor disagreement. Given the nature of the man, surely Sir Charles would have made more enemies over the years? Why had they not been mentioned? Russell's name had come far too easily. Were Sir Charles and Brockway suggesting Russell whilst avoiding more serious contenders? There was no way of knowing at present. Nevertheless Ravenscroft resolved that he would seek out Russell, but first he needed to explore Hill Court in more detail. Old houses sometimes contained dark secrets. Often the servants were the custodians of these past secrets. He would begin with them.

Opening a door at the far end of the entrance hall, he found himself in a corridor, the door of which in turn opened into what he deemed to be a kind of dining-room. Here a fine set of hunting prints and numerous items of brass and copper were hung from the walls. The door at the far end of the room revealed another short passage that lead into the kitchens.

'Ah Inspector Ravenscroft, good morning to you, sir. Is there any news of Miss Chilton?'

Ravenscroft recognised Jukes, the servant who had accompanied them to the churchyard the previous evening.

'Good morning. No, we have nothing to report. But I see I am disturbing you both,' replied Ravenscroft noticing also a plump, rosy-cheeked elderly woman seated at the kitchen table.

'It is quite all right, sir. We usually have some refreshment at this time of day,' said Jukes.

'Please continue, Mr Jukes.'

'May I introduce you to Mrs Greenway our cook.'

'Mrs Greenway I am pleased to make your acquaintance. I wonder whether I might ask to join you for some refreshment? I must say it was rather chilly by the banks of the Salwarpe this morning.'

'Of course, sir. Sit yourself down there by the stove. You'll soon get warm there,' said the cook in a cheery manner rising from the table.

'Sir Charles does not usually encourage us to speak to folk from upstairs,' said Jukes.

'Well I won't tell him, if you don't,' smiled Ravenscroft, accepting the seat and rubbing his hands near the stove.

'Would you like a cup of tea, Mr Ravenscroft?' asked the cook.

'That would be most welcome, Mrs Greenway.'

The cook walked over to the dresser, took down a cup and saucer from the rack and returned to the table. 'This will soon warm you up sir,' she said pouring out the liquid from a large teapot. 'Please help yourself to milk and sugar.'

'You are most generous. My word, this is excellent tea,' said Ravenscroft after he had sampled the brew.

'Mrs Greenway makes the best tea in all of Worcestershire,' proclaimed Jukes.

'I can more than believe it,' said Ravenscroft taking another sip.

'Get away with you, Jukes. Perhaps you would care to sample a piece of my special homemade fruit cake, Inspector?' smiled the cook.

'Delighted I'm sure,' replied Ravenscroft. 'If it is half as good as the tea, I will consider myself to be a fortunate man.'

The cook cut a piece from the cake which adorned a china stand on the dresser, and placed it upon a blue patterned plate before handing it to the detective.

Jukes and the cook looked at Ravenscroft anxiously as he took a bite.

'Mrs Greenway, this is just the best fruit cake I have ever eaten in all my life!' exclaimed Ravenscroft. 'Mr Jukes, you must be a happy man?'

'Indeed I am sir,' smiled the servant. 'Mrs Greenway takes good care of us all. We servants want for nothing.'

'Excellent, my dear lady,' added Ravenscroft after swallowing another mouthful.

'The recipe was handed down to me by my late grandmother, and she always claimed that it had been given to her by her grandmother, who said it had been given to her by a cook who worked for good Queen Anne!' proclaimed the cook.

'Well, what is good for Queen Anne is certainly more than welcome to me. You must let my wife have the recipe. I suppose you must have worked for Sir Charles and Lady Chilton for a number of years?' inquired Ravenscroft.

'For the past fifteen years sir.'

'And you, Mister Jukes?' continued Ravenscroft.

'About ten years, but you were here before Sir Charles, were you not, Mrs Greenway?'

'Yes. I was here when Master Peter was here — and before him when Master Christopher was the owner,' replied the cook replenishing Ravenscroft's cup.

'Forgive me, but what relation were these gentlemen to Sir Charles?' asked Ravenscroft interested in gaining all he could from the lady.

'Sir Christopher were the father of Sir Charles and Master Peter. He was a real gentleman. Always asking after the servants' welfare. Nothing was too much trouble. Looked after us all proper he did. There was always a generous present at Christmas there was. Master Peter was his eldest son, and he was a lovely man, but then he had been such a good child, so kind and gentle, a really loving child if you get my meaning,' said the cook warming to her subject.

'And what happened to Sir Christopher and Master Peter?'

'Died sir. About ten years ago it was. Master Peter died suddenly. He went away one day on business to London and caught a fever there by all accounts. His death broke his father's heart. He never go over it. Died himself a few months afterwards. They're both buried in the churchyard yonder.'

'How very sad,' sympathized Ravenscroft. 'So Sir Charles took over the business then?'

'He did indeed,' said Jukes leaning back in his chair.

'And how do you find Sir Charles?'

'"Find" sir?' asked Jukes.

'Yes, how do you find Sir Charles — is he an easy master to work for?'

'Not for us to say, sir,' said the servant defensively.

'I quite understand your reluctance to talk about your master. I appreciate that. Loyalty is to be commended in a servant these days.'

'Master can be a bit hard at times,' said the cook. 'He likes to run a tight ship, if you get my drift.'

'I am sure he does. And Lady Chilton?'

'Ah, now she is totally different. I've never met a kinder woman, the poor soul,' nodded the cook.

'Oh, why do you say that?' asked Ravenscroft thankful that his easy line of questioning was at last beginning to bring forth encouraging results.

'Not well. Stays in her room all day now. She sees no one except for the family and Doctor Staple. No one can find what's wrong with her,' continued Mrs Greenway.

'I am sorry to hear that. Has Lady Chilton been ill for long?'

'For past year I'd say, wouldn't you say so, Mrs Greenway,' said Jukes.

'As long as that, Mr Jukes? Well yes, I suppose it must be.'

'How long have Sir Charles and Lady Chilton been married?' asked Ravenscroft.

'For nearly nine years I'd say. Of course she was betrothed to Master Peter first. They made a lovely couple. So much in love. But then, as we said, he died so unexpected. A great tragedy it was sir.'

'A bit like Catherine of Aragon,' suggested Ravenscroft.

'Catherine of Aragon?', asked Jukes.

'Yes, you know, Jukes, she married Henry VIII, after first being betrothed to his elder brother,' offered Mrs Greenway.'

'Is Miss Mildred their only child?' asked Ravenscroft.

'Yes sir.'

'Would you say that she is a happy child? Is she well cared for by her parents?' asked Ravenscroft becoming more intrigued.

'Why yes sir. Her mother adores her. Cannot do enough for her. I sometimes think that she only lives for her daughter. She is very distraught by all this, sir. I fears for her sanity I does. She is so fragile. It is all so very sad. Would you like some more cake, Mister Ravenscroft?' said the cook.

'I would indeed, but I fear I must not give in to temptation, good as it is,' laughed Ravenscroft. 'What do you make of Miss Petterson, the governess?'

'Bit stuck up, if you ask me. She don't like socializing with us servants. She thinks we be all daddaky to her,' said Mrs Greenway rubbing the side of her nose with her finger.

'Daddaky?' asked Ravenscroft.

'Daddaky. Thinks we are all completely inferior to her, being staff,' explained the cook.

'And how does Miss Petterson get on with her charge?'

'Well enough I suppose.'

'There have been no arguments, or fallings out between them?'

'None as I know of.'

'Have either of you seen any suspicious strangers in the neighbourhood recently?'

'None that I can think of,' replied the cook.

'No, none,' added Jukes.

'Well, thank you Mrs Greenway, and you too Mr Jukes,' said Ravenscroft standing up from the table. 'You have both been very helpful. The cake and tea were most welcome.'

'I'll let you have that recipe, Inspector,' said the cook.

'Thank you Mrs Greenway, I look forward to that. In the meantime I wish you both good day.'

* * *

Ravenscroft retraced his steps through the dining-room and hall, pausing to look at the family portraits on the walls, before deciding to make his way slowly up the imposing curved marble staircase. Finding himself on the upper landing he looked through a large window at the stable buildings and fields which stretched out below him, before turning to admire the large number of books inside a glass-fronted bookcase.

A faint sobbing sound somewhere in the distance made him look up quickly from the book he had taken down from one of the shelves. He stood still listening to the plaintive cries for some moments, until they ceased as suddenly as they had begun. Ravenscroft wondered who had made the mournful sound — could they have been uttered by the missing girl? And if so, would he find her locked in one of rooms that lead off the landing?

Replacing the volume, he made his way over to one of the doors, and gently tapped on the woodwork. Receiving no reply, he cautiously opened the door a few inches, and stepped gingerly into the room.

'Forgive me. I heard crying,' said Ravenscroft, addressing the figure who stood before the window in the semi-darkened interior.

'Who . . . who are you?' said the woman turning round to face him.

'Inspector Ravenscroft, Lady Chilton. We spoke last night when I arrived,' said Ravenscroft standing by the door and feeling somewhat reticent to proceed further.

'Ravenscroft?'

'Yes, I came about your daughter.'

'My daughter? Mildred. Have you found her? Please say you have found her, and that all is well?' said the distraught woman coming forward to meet him and clasping his hands tightly in hers.

'No, we have not found your daughter yet, Lady Chilton, but we are trying everything we can. I am sure it will not be long before you are reunited,' said Ravenscroft trying to sound as reassuring as he could.

'My daughter! My poor daughter!' cried the woman, her sad eyes filling once more with tears.

'Please do not distress yourself, Lady Chilton. May I help you to a seat? A glass of water perhaps?'

'Ravenscroft you say. Yes, of course, Ravenscroft. The man who has come to find my daughter. You must forgive me. Please do take a seat,' said Lady Chilton attempting to regain her composure, whilst leading the detective over to a small sofa.

'Thank you,' replied Ravenscroft accepting the seat, and observing that his hostess seemed reluctant to relinquish her tight grip on his right hand, as she sat down beside him.

'Will you ever find her, my poor daughter? 'she said looking into his eyes.

'Of course, of that I am sure.'

'But how can you be so certain?' asked Lady Chilton anxiously.

'In my experience missing children are usually found alive and well after a day or two,' replied Ravenscroft knowing that he was lying, as he looked into the worn face full of tears and sorrows.

'She is all I have in this world you know. There is no one else now. For such a long time there has been no one. I could not live without her — quite alone.'

'You have your husband. He must be a great comfort to you?'

'My husband?'

'Yes, Sir Charles.'

'My husband has little time for me. He is always busy with his work.'

'I see.'

'I am quite alone . . . quite alone . . . there is no one to help me . . .' continued the woman, her voice trailing away as she looked vacantly past Ravenscroft.

'Can you think of anyone who could have taken your daughter?'

'Taken? But surely she is lost, not taken?'

'Mr Russell?' suggested Ravenscroft.

'Mr Russell? I do not understand. She is lost, poor Mildred is lost. My poor daughter is out there somewhere. I must go to her, she may be sick, she may be injured, she may have need of me. Yes I must go to her,' said Lady Chilton relinquishing Ravenscroft's hand as she rose quickly from the sofa.

'I don't think that would be wise—' interjected Ravenscroft.

'But she is out there, all alone . . . she is looking for me . . . all alone'. Again the voice trailed off to an almost inaudible whisper, as the speaker sank down despondently onto a nearby chair and covered her face with her hands.

Ravenscroft sat silently, sharing the mother's distress, wanting to utter words that would bring comfort, but knowing that anything he would say could be of little use. Instead he distracted himself by looking around the small drawing-room, with its simple furniture, half-drawn curtains and writing table. An open book, a glass of water and a pair of spectacles lay on the side-table near the sofa. To Ravenscroft it seemed the kind of room that a lady would seek to avoid as much as possible, rather than a room where one would wish to spend one's daylight hours.

Then he observed the photograph of a young girl, mounted within a silver frame, that was placed on a small table at the opposite end of the sofa. Ravenscroft recalled that the smiling portrait of the girl with the ringlets was a copy of the same picture, which had been given to him by the governess the previous evening, and wondered what dangers she might now be facing.

'Mildred,' whispered Lady Chilton. 'Such a beautiful girl.'

'She is a credit to you, ma'am.'

'Such a comfort to me. A memory of the past. We must cling to the past.'

'I am sure we will be able to find her.'

'You have children, Mr Ravenscroft?' asked Lady Chilton, after some moments had elapsed.

'I have two. Both boys. My wife and I have been most fortunate,' replied Ravenscroft, grateful that the quietness of the room had been broken.

'Two boys . . . I should have liked a boy . . . Mildred is my daughter.' Again the sorrowful voice trailed away to nothing, as its owner's eyes stared vacantly down at the carpet.

'Lady Chilton, I must take my leave of you now. Rest assured that I will find your daughter. I give you that promise. As soon as I have some news I will let you know,' said Ravenscroft, realizing that he could do no more, and rose quickly to his feet.

'All alone . . . she is all alone you know . . . all alone . . .'

'I will return, Lady Chilton. I wish you good day.'

'Yes . . . return.'

As Ravenscroft let himself quietly out of the room, he gave a backward glance at the forlorn figure, and felt sickening anxiety within him.

* * *

'Well Tom, how was your morning?' asked Ravenscroft as the two men walked away from Hill Court.

'I sent the telegram addressed to Lord and Lady Roberts of Warminster enquiring about the governess,' replied Crabb.

'Good. I think we need to know a lot more about our Miss Petterson.'

'Then I made a few discreet enquiries regarding Sir Charles in the shops and inns in the town. It seems he is not particularly liked in the area. Bit of a hard taskmaster by all accounts, used to getting his own way.'

'That is what we surmised.'

'He also has quite a reputation for meanness.'

'That is the impression I gained from talking to the servants. Apparently he inherited the family business from his father about ten years ago. There was an elder brother, but he died before the father.'

'People speak well of his wife, although she has not been seen in the town for nearly a year now. There are all sorts of rumours flying around about her. Her memory has broken down, some say; bedridden after an accident, others claim. But I expect it is all idle gossip,' continued Crabb.

'Well I have managed to speak with Lady Chilton, and she is indeed a sorrowful figure, but how much her present state of mind is due to the sudden loss of her daughter, or to a more deep seated ailment, I can't judge, but I tell you one thing Crabb, my heart went out to the poor woman. We must do all we can to find her daughter,' said Ravenscroft with determination.

'I also made enquiries at the Gardeners Arms, but they saw nothing yesterday.'

'Thank you, Tom.'

'What else did you learn, sir?'

'I spoke with that Brockway fellow. Can't say I like the man. He was not very forthcoming and certainly did not want me to see Lady Chilton. He gave me this long list of people who have had dealings with Sir Charles. When I pressed him for anyone in particular who might bare a grudge against Chilton, he reluctantly came up with a James Russell.'

'Who is he, sir?' asked Crabb.

'A local farmer. Apparently Sir Charles wanted to buy some land from him, but Mr Russell declined the offer, and there were sharp words between the two. Russell has salt deposits on his land; that was why Chilton wanted it. So we shall make our way there now and see what this Mr Russell has to say about the matter,' replied Ravenscroft frowning and rubbing his chest.

'Oh one more thing sir. As I was returning to the house, I observed that the church was open, so I went inside and found the vicar there. He told me that when he has chosen the hymns for the following Sunday, he usually puts the numbers of the hymns on the marker boards.'

'So that would seem to confirm the governess's story about going into the church.'

'Not quite sir. The reverend has not yet chosen the hymns for next Sunday's service.'

'So she was deceiving us,' said Ravenscroft pulling a face.

'Are you all right, sir? You look a bit peaky, if you don't mind my saying so,' said a concerned Crabb.

'Indigestion, Tom. Indigestion through eating the most awful fruit cake I have ever tasted. Queen Anne has a lot to answer for,' grumbled Ravenscroft.

'Queen Anne?'

'Never mind, Tom. I will tell you some other time. Let's go and see this Mr Russell.'

* * *

A short walk down the hill and along Vines Lane bought the two policemen out into the surrounding countryside.

'I believe that must be Mr Russell's farm over there,' said Ravenscroft pointing to a collection of buildings in the distance.

Crabb opened a gate and they walked across a long field towards the main building. As they neared, a slim, middle-aged man dressed in a well-worn checked suit appeared; he wore a deerstalker hat, and carried a shotgun under his arm and stepped forward to meet them.

'Good day sir. I am looking for Mr Russell,' said Ravenscroft observing that the man had a long narrow scar down one side of his face.

'You've found him — and who might you be?' asked the man defensively eyeing the detectives.

'I am Detective Inspector Ravenscroft and this is my colleague Constable Crabb.'

'Ah, you must be looking for that lost girl, young Miss Chilton,' replied the farmer.

'We are indeed,' replied Ravenscroft.

'Well she is not here, I can tell you. Searched all the barns and sheds myself this morning.'

'How did you learn Miss Chilton was missing?'

'The news was all over the town this morning.'

'And you searched your buildings in response? Did you think that she might have made her own way here?' inquired Ravenscroft.

'No. The church is a good mile from my house. Rather a long way for a girl to have wandered out here on her own, I would have thought,' replied the farmer in a casual way.

'But nevertheless you thought it necessary to examine your buildings?'

'Look, I don't know what you are implying, Inspector—' began Russell.

'I am not implying anything, sir. I am merely curious to know why you took the trouble to search your outbuildings, knowing that it was unlikely that the girl would be there,' continued Ravenscroft.

'Well she could have come here, I suppose. That is why I searched the buildings. Look if that is all, I need to get on. I've a lot to attend to today. If the girl should turn up I will of course inform you of the fact,' said the farmer abruptly turning away.

'We understand that you and Sir Charles have recently had a falling out,' said Ravenscroft quickly.

'Ah, I see. You have come about my land. Chilton thinks there is a potential salt mine underneath this field. Wants to uncover it and add it to his empire. I told him it was not for sale and sent him packing.'

'And how did Sir Charles react?'

'Well he didn't like it, did he!' said Russell raising his voice. 'He's used to having his own way. Thinks he can buy up the whole town, and countryside for miles around, and all the folks as well. Well I told him he was not to be so humoured. My ancestors have farmed this land for the past five generations, and there is no way that I will be selling any of it to that jumped up, loud-mouthed, intimidating bully. That's all I've got to say. Now good day to you,' replied Russell placing his shot gun on his shoulder.

'So you have not taken his daughter then, sir?' called out Crabb.

'Good day to you!' replied Russell, glowering at the constable, before turning on his heel and striding off towards his farm at a brisk pace.

'I think Tom, that we might have annoyed our Mr Russell,' said Ravenscroft retracing his steps out of the field.

'He could have the girl tied up in one of those old barns?' suggested Crabb.

'He could, but you are forgetting one thing Tom — why would Russell have taken the girl? What reason would he have had to have done so?'

'Perhaps he hated Sir Charles and took the girl to get his own back. He's got a bit of a hot temper, I'd say.'

'Does not seem likely, although I would agree with you that there appears to be no love lost between the two men,' replied Ravenscroft.

'He could be holding the girl for a day or so before making a demand for money for her return?'

'Maybe, but until we receive such a demand we will not know. Now that we have made the acquaintance of Mr Russell, let us return to the canal and see whether the men have found anything there.'

* * *

'Anything to report?' asked Ravenscroft as he and Crabb neared the canal bank.

'Just this, sir. One of the men found it floating down there,' replied the constable passing over a piece of material to his superior officer. 'Could be the girl's handkerchief?'

'You could be correct, constable. White with red roses embroidered round the edge,' said Ravenscroft examining the item. 'And see here the letter "M".'

'Mildred Chilton?' offered Crabb.

'Take charge of it, Tom. This is valuable evidence. We will make enquiries at the house to see if it's owner was indeed the young lady. I take it that you found nothing else, constable?'

'No sir. We've gone up to the lock gates in either direction, but there is no trace of the girl.'

'And the river?'

'Nothing there either, sir.'

'The girl could have dropped it into canal on another occasion?' suggested Crabb.

'Yes. That could have been the case. Miss Petterson should be able to tell us whether Miss Chilton had this handkerchief in her possession on the day she disappeared,' said Ravenscroft.

'Begging your pardon sir, we have made quite an extensive search in either direction along the railway, river and canal, but do you want us to widen the search area?' asked the constable.

'No, I think you and the men have done your best. I'm sure that if the girl ran away from the churchyard and met with a serious accident down here, we would have found her remains by now. It seems more and more likely that she was taken against her will. Stand down the men, constable.'

'Right sir.'

'Well Tom, I think it is time we returned once more to Hill Court. Sir Charles may have returned there by now, and we also need to have further words with the governess concerning her visit to the church,' said Ravenscroft moving away from the canal.

'I think someone over there is trying to attract our attention sir,' said Crabb. 'Over here boy!'

A postboy ran towards them along the bank of the canal. 'Telegram for Ravenscroft! Telegram for Ravenscroft!' he called out.

'I am Ravenscroft. Thank you,' replied the detective taking the envelope and giving the youth a coin. 'Looks as though we have a reply from Lord and Lady Roberts of Warminster to our enquiry regarding the governess. Well I'm blessed! This certainly throws a different complexion on the case.'

'What sir?' asked Crabb.

'It seems, Tom, that our Miss Petterson died five years ago!'

CHAPTER FOUR

LEDBURY

'Please ma'am, there's a young lady who would like a word with you.'

'Thank you Susan. Did you tell her that Mr Ravenscroft is away at present,' replied Lucy without looking up from her needlework.

'Yes ma'am but she says she must see someone, and I thought you might wish to help her.'

'I think it would be better if she called when Mr Ravenscroft is at home.'

'I've told her that, but she is most insistent that she sees you. She seems quite distressed, ma'am.'

'Then I think you had better show her in, Susan,' said Lucy placing her sewing down on the small table at the side of her chair.

'Miss Corbett,' announced the maid returning a few moments later.

'Miss Corbett, I'm afraid my husband is not at home at present,' said Lucy rising from her seat and looking across at the forlorn figure who had just entered her living-room.

'I'm sorry to have disturbed you ma'am, but I had to see someone,' said the young woman suddenly bursting into tears.

'My dear Miss Corbett, please do not distress yourself,' said Lucy coming forward and placing an arm on the new arrival's shoulder. 'Do take a seat on the sofa. Susan, will you bring a glass of water for the young lady. Whatever is the matter?'

'I'm sorry ma'am. It's my baby, my poor Lily!' sobbed the woman accepting the seat and drawing her shawl closer round her head.

'Your baby?'

'She has gone! She is not there. They have taken her away!'

'Someone has taken your baby?' asked Lucy sitting down beside the visitor.

'They said she would be looked after. They promised me that she would have the best of everything,' continued the woman, tears falling down her face.

'There now, pray do not distress yourself, Miss Corbett. Here, drink this water,' said Lucy handing her the glass of liquid, that the maid had just brought into the room.

'Thank you ma'am. You are most kind.'

'And when you have drunk that, you shall tell me all about it,' said Lucy reassuringly.

'Thank you.'

'Now Miss Corbett, I cannot keep calling you Miss Corbett. What is your first name?' asked Lucy after a few moments had elapsed.

'Alice.'

'And where do you live Alice?'

'I work at Brewster's Farm out at Wellington Heath.'

'And what do you do there?'

'I am a milkmaid, ma'am,' replied the young woman gradually recovering her composure and turning back the shawl from her head.

'And how long have you worked at Wellington Heath?'

'Three months ma'am.'

'And where were you before that?'

The woman hesitated for a moment and drew back, before eventually replying. 'Hanbury near Droitwich.'

'How long has your baby, Lily, been missing?'

'Three months, Mrs Ravenscroft.'

'Three months!' replied Lucy somewhat taken aback. 'Why on earth did you not report the matter sooner?'

'Oh she wasn't taken then.'

'I think perhaps you should start at the beginning,' suggested Lucy looking perplexed.

'I'll try and explain, ma'am. It was while I was working on the farm at Hanbury. It were those soldiers. They were camping out near the farm for two weeks. He said he would take care of me, but then he was gone with the rest of them, and I was with his child — and I did not know where he had gone.'

'I see,' said Lucy turning away.

'Do not think bad of me, ma'am. He said he loved me; said he would marry me, and that everything would be right with us.'

'I do not think badly of you, Alice. You were young and no doubt easily lead astray. I more than comprehend your situation. Men can be so feckless,' said the older woman placing her hand on the other's arm.

'You understand, Mrs Ravenscroft,' replied Alice looking sadly into Lucy's eyes.

'Tell me what happened?' asked Lucy quickly seeking to change the nature of her questioning.

'They were very good to me at Hanbury. Said I could stay on until after the baby came. Then when she was born, I decided to call her Lily.'

'That is a very pretty name.'

'There was a pond on the farm, and I thought the lilies looked so beautiful there. So peaceful and quiet. Then a few weeks after Lily had been born, the farmer said I would have to leave. Said the baby was always crying and they didn't want the other servants disturbed. I was desperate. I had nowhere to go,' said Alice tears again forming in her large eyes.

'Had you no parents, or brothers or sisters? Someone who could look after you and the baby?'

'No ma'am. My father died when I was quite young, and my mother married another who did not want me. That's why I had left home all those years ago. I was so desperate!' she sobbed.

'There, take another drink of the water.'

'Thank you ma'am, you are very kind. They said either the baby would have to go, or we would have to leave together. I did not know what to do. Then I saw the advertisement in the local newspaper. The Droitwich Guardian. It said that a lady had just lost her baby, and was anxious to take on another, and bring the child up as her own.'

'I see. So you replied to this advertisement?'

'Yes. She seemed such a nice lady. Told me in her letter how she and her husband lived in a fine house in Cheltenham, how very sad they were that the Lord had taken away their only child. When I wrote and told them all about Lily, they said God had answered their prayers, and that they would do everything they could to see that my baby would have a good life, if I would agree to let them have her. They said I would still be able to visit her as often as I could. So I took her to the railway station and gave away my darling Lily!'

'There, there, do not distress yourself so,' said Lucy placing her arm round the shoulders of the sobbing girl. 'You did what you thought best for your child. You have nothing to reproach yourself with. I have no doubt that you were acting in your child's best interests. Any other young mother in your situation would have done the same.'

'Thank you ma'am, but I don't deserve your words of kindness. What kind of mother would give away her own baby?'

'A mother who was desperate to do all she could for her child. It seems as though this couple were very Christian in their actions. Did they not require anything from you in return for their generosity?'

'The lady said her husband wanted five pounds to help towards the costs of Lily's upbringing.'

'Five pounds is rather a lot of money.'

'I had a few pounds put by, sold the old ring I had, and the farmer gave me some towards the amount, he was very good, but said I would have to go elsewhere and find work. They did not want the disgrace on the farm. I did not want my baby taken away ma'am, and put in the workhouse.'

'Of course not. So you met this woman and her husband at the railway station and gave her five pounds. What happened next?'

'She took away my darling Lily,' sobbed Alice.

'That must have been very distressing for you, but at least you had the reassurance that your daughter was being looked after by these kind people, and that you were free to visit her at any time?'

'That's what I thought, ma'am. She said I should wait six months before I could come and visit Lily. Give her time to settle in, she said. But I missed her so much. You understand that, Mrs Ravenscroft?'

'Of course; that is only natural; you are her mother.'

'So last week I went to their house in Cheltenham, but when I knocked on the door the servant came out, and told me that there was no one by the name of Huddlestone living there, and that there had never been anyone living there with that name.'

'Perhaps you went to the wrong house?' suggested Lucy.

'No Mrs Ravenscroft, it was the right house. 22 Suffolk Square in Montpellier, Cheltenham. That is what she told me, and that is the address that was on the letter.'

'Do you still have the letter?'

'Yes ma'am,' replied Alice reaching into her pocket and retrieving a folded sheet of blue paper.

'Do you still have the envelope?'

'No ma'am.'

Lucy read aloud the letter—

22 Suffolk Square,
Cheltenham.

3rd November 1889.

My Dear Miss Corbett,
Thank you so much for your letter.
My husband and I were very touched by your story, and are
looking forward so much to seeing both you and little Lily.
I thank the day the good Lord bought us together!
Now, to our arrangements:
Please bring Lily to Droitwich railway station on Thursday
afternoon. Mr Huddlestone and I will meet you on the
platform at three o'clock. Do not forget the items that we
discussed.
We have so much we can give Lily.
God bless you, my dear!
You are our salvation.

Your good friend,
Amelia Huddlestone.

'I am sorry, I threw away the envelope. Tell me, Mrs Ravenscroft, what have they done with my Lily? Why were they not there when I went to the house? If something terrible has happened to her, I shall never forgive myself! To think that I have given away my baby!'

'There now, Alice, do not be alarmed. I am sure that there must be a sensible explanation for all this. I will have a word with my husband when he returns from Droitwich tonight, and we will go together to Cheltenham sometime in the near future and make enquiries on your behalf.'

'Oh, thank you ma'am. I am so besides myself with worry. I would be so grateful to you and the Inspector.'

'Can you tell me what this Mrs Huddlestone looked like?'

'She was thin, with grey hair, probably around forty in years and she spoke in a strange kind of voice, soft and musical it were. I could tell, though that she wasn't from around these parts. Her voice was different.'

'May I keep the letter?' asked Lucy rising from her seat. 'Yes ma'am.'

'Did you give this Mrs Huddlestone anything else besides the five pounds?'

'She asked that I give her all of Lily's clothes. I did not have much. I wrapped her in a red shawl.'

'Now you leave the matter with us. I'm sure that my husband will be able to get to the bottom of this. He is very good at solving mysteries,' smiled Lucy.

'Oh thank you, Mrs Ravenscroft,' said Alice drawing her shawl over her head once more as she rose from the sofa.

'As I said, my husband is investigating a case over in Droitwich at the moment, so it may be a few days before he can go to Cheltenham.'

'I understand ma'am. I cannot thank you enough,' replied Alice.

'Now you are not to worry,' said Lucy reassuringly placing her fingers on the girl's hand. 'As soon as we have any news we will let you know. Brewster's farm at Wellington Heath, I think you said?'

'Yes ma'am. Oh thank you so much, Mrs Ravenscroft. You have put my mind at ease.'

'Susan, will you show Miss Corbett out please.'

Lucy watched as her visitor left the room, then she sat down on the chair deep in thought.

'The poor woman,' said Susan returning to the room. 'To think she had to give up that poor mite.'

'Yes Susan, it is a very sad state of affairs. She must have been desperate to surrender her young child in such a fashion.'

'Still I suppose Mr Ravenscroft will soon be able to get to the bottom of it.'

'Yes, I expect so — although I think he will be very busy in Droitwich for the rest of the day.'

'The poor woman,' repeated the maid shaking her head. 'Pity we could not help her sooner, Mrs Ravenscroft.'

Lucy thought deeply for a moment.

'Susan, fetch me Bradshaws. Let us see when the next train leaves for Cheltenham. Would you mind looking after Master Richard and Master Arthur for the rest of the day — and then looking out my new grey coat and hat?'

* * *

Later that afternoon Lucy turned away from the busy area of Montpellier with its eloquent buildings, wide roads, horse-drawn vehicles and busy shoppers, and found herself walking down a secluded tree-lined road. After going on some steps, the road abruptly opened out into a strangely quiet oasis of calm, that declared itself to be Suffolk Square. Here the rows of five storey houses gazed sedately at one another from opposite sides of the square. The late afternoon sun shone fitfully on the spacious pavements, as a light breeze blew the remnants of last year's leaves along the road. Lucy could see three small boys were engaged in a game of hide and seek behind the railings of a small enclosed park, from where a young woman was visible, gently pushing a pram back and forth beneath the trees.

Removing the blue folded paper from her purse and reading the address once more, Lucy made her way past several buildings, until she reached a brass plate with the number 22 neatly engraved into its surface. She reached out and raised the ornate knocker, but before she could bring it down upon the wood, she found the door suddenly opening before her.

'Good afternoon. I wonder if Mrs Huddlestone is at home?'

'I'm afraid you must have the wrong address miss. This is number 22,' replied the young housemaid.

'No, I believe I have the correct address. I was told that Mr and Mrs Huddlestone resided here.'

'You are mistaken, miss. This house belongs to Miss Jameson and her sister.'

'And how long have they lived here?' persisted Lucy.

'For nearly thirty years I believe; long before I came.'

'I see. Perhaps you know of someone else with the name of Huddlestone who lives in the square?' asked Lucy hopefully.

'I'm sorry miss, I know of no one in this neighbourhood called Huddlestone, although there was a young girl, now I think about it, who knocked on the door last week, who was asking to see the same person,' replied the housemaid, a puzzled expression on her face.

'I wonder if it might be possible to speak to your mistress?'

'I don't know about that, miss. Mistress is not taken to receiving unannounced visitors.'

'It is a very urgent matter. I would be very much obliged,' pleaded Lucy.

'Well I suppose I could ask, miss.'

'Thank you,' smiled Lucy.

'Whom shall I say is calling?'

'My name is Mrs Ravenscroft. My husband is a police inspector.'

'If you would just wait here, ma'am,' said the maid closing the door.

Lucy looked across the square towards the drab, austere church hall and wondered whether she had been somewhat impetuous in her decision to seek out the Huddlestones of Cheltenham. Perhaps it would have been wiser to have consulted her husband first, and to have allowed him to make enquiries? That would have been the more prudent course, but the unexpected events of earlier that day had prompted her to bring about a swift reunion between the unfortunate young woman and her abandoned child. The address at the top of the letter had clearly stated number 22 Suffolk Square, and yet no one of that name appeared to reside in the vicinity. All she could do was hope that the owner of the property would allow her to call unannounced, and that such an interview would furnish the information she was so anxious to obtain.

'Miss Jameson says you may call upon her,' announced the maid.

'Thank you.'

'If you would care to follow me, ma'am.'

Lucy followed the maid across the hall and into a spacious drawing room, where she found herself standing in front of two elderly ladies.

'Mrs Ravenscroft, ma'am,' announced the maid.

'Mrs Ravenscroft,' said one of the ladies coming forwards to meet her. 'Florence Jameson. How can my sister and I be of assistance to you?'

'I am sorry for the intrusion ladies. I was under the impression that a Mrs Huddlestone resided here.'

'I believe that our maid has already informed you that there has never been anyone of that name who has resided here. My sister and I have lived here for over thirty years.'

'So I believe. Perhaps I might explain the reason for my visit?' asked Lucy somewhat nervously.

'Then you had best take a seat, Mrs Ravenscroft. Can we offer you some refreshment?' said the other elderly lady.

'No, thank you,' replied Lucy seating herself on the chair Miss Jameson indicated.

'I understand that your husband is a police inspector?' enquired the first speaker.

'Yes. We reside in Ledbury. My husband would have come in person to see you, but he has been called away on urgent business to Droitwich.'

'So you have chosen to come in his place?' smiled the second sister.

'It is rather a delicate matter. Earlier today, ladies, a young woman called upon me at home and told me a rather distressing story — of how under pressing circumstances, she gave away her infant daughter to a person of the name Huddlestone, whom she believed resided at this address.'

'Gave away her daughter!' exclaimed the two sisters, speaking almost in unison.

'I am sorry, ladies, I did not mean to cause alarm.'

'I think you had better explain as soon as possible, Mrs Ravenscroft.'

'Yes, of course.'

During the following few minutes, Lucy recounted in full the detailed events of earlier that day.

'What an extraordinary story!' said one of the sisters.

'So you understand, ladies, why I felt it necessary to call upon you. I felt I had to do all I could to reunite this poor woman with her daughter.'

'It is indeed a very sad account you have presented to us, Mrs Ravenscroft, and although my sister and I have a great deal of sympathy for the young lady in question, and also commend you for your admirable concern, we nevertheless do not see how we can be of any assistance to you in this matter. As already stated, we have lived in this house for over thirty years and have never met anyone of the name of Huddlestone in all that time.'

'I see,' said Lucy looking dispiritedly at the neatly folded hands in her lap.

'May we see the letter you mentioned?'

'Of course.'

'Ah, I see that our address has indeed been hand written at the top of the notepaper. If you would care to follow me, Mrs Ravenscroft, across to the bureau.'

Lucy rose from her chair and walked over to the writing desk.

'You will see that all our notepaper has the address clearly printed at the heading of each sheet, so your letter could not possibly have been written here. It would seem that the writer of your letter must have written it elsewhere.'

'So it would seem, ladies.'

'Perhaps we could consult the local directory, sister, there may be a Huddlestone listed under another address,' suggested the other Jameson sister.

The first sister opened a red covered book that lay on top of the bureau and handed it to Lucy.

'It would seem, ladies, that Miss Corbett has been given the incorrect information,' said Lucy after a few moments of turning over the pages. 'There is certainly no one of that name who resides in the town.'

'Dear me,' said the other sister sympathetically. 'What will you do now, Mrs Ravenscroft?'

'I must confess, ladies, that I am at a loss. Why this Mrs Huddlestone should have given this address to poor Miss Corbett, I do not know. It seems that we have been cruelly deceived. Perhaps my husband will know how to proceed further in this matter. I must apologize for calling upon you ladies so unexpectedly, and thank you both for your time and concern,' said Lucy feeling embarrassed, and anxious to leave as quickly as she could.

'I am sorry, Mrs Ravenscroft, that neither my sister nor I could throw any light upon this strange affair. I hope that you will be able to reunite mother and child.'

'Yes — I thank you again, ladies. Good day.'

A few minutes later, as Lucy made her way along the streets of Montpelier towards the railway station, she was overcome with feelings of inadequacy and disappointment. When she had set out on her journey from Ledbury earlier that afternoon, it was with the expectation of discovering Mrs Huddlestone and the infant child at the house in Suffolk Square, and of eventually being able to reunite both mother and child. But now that she had learnt the awful truth, that the woman who had taken the child had clearly lied about her circumstances, Lucy now found herself returning home with a sense of foreboding and anxiety. Worse still, she now had to explain to an anxious mother that her journey had been in vain.

CHAPTER FIVE

DROITWICH

'Sir Charles will see you now, Inspector.'

'Thank you, Mr Brockway.'

Ravenscroft and Crabb had returned to Hill Court, and after waiting in the hall for a few minutes, were about to be admitted into the study.

'Ah Ravenscroft, I suppose you have no news of my daughter?' asked Chilton looking up from some papers that lay before him on his desk, as they entered the room.

'We have made extensive searches of the railway line, river bank and canal towpaths and there is no sign of your daughter, Sir Charles,' replied Ravenscroft.

'I suppose that must be something. Now look here, Ravenscroft, I'm damned displeased with you, man!' growled Chilton.

'I am sorry, sir,' said Ravenscroft taken aback by the sudden outburst. 'I assure you, sir, that we are doing all we can to find your daughter.'

'No, not that, man. Going behind my back and talking to my wife without my permission. A gross intrusion of privacy!'

'Forgive me sir, but—' began Ravenscroft.

'No, sir, I will not forgive you. My wife is of a delicate disposition. This business has upset her tremendously. She is devoted to my daughter. I thought I had clearly informed you that she was indisposed.'

'Sir Charles, if I am to solve this case and bring your child safely back to Hill Court, it is imperative that I question everyone I can, and that includes your wife,' protested Ravenscroft feeling increasingly discomforted by the baronet's anger.

'The servants said you intruded into my wife's dressing-room, completely unannounced!'

'I was walking on the landing, Sir Charles, when I heard what I thought was crying, and thinking that someone was in distress I opened one of the doors—'

'Damn it man, you had no right! No right at all! I shall have words with your superior,' threatened Chilton banging a fist down on the desk before him. 'We will ask someone else to take over the case.'

'I am sorry, Sir Charles. I have no desire to cause any members of your family any more distress. As I said, I heard crying, and thought it my duty to investigate. The cries might have originated from your daughter, whom I thought might be trapped inside one of the rooms. I did not know at the time that it was your wife who was on the other side of the door. I can assure you that once I had exchanged a few words with Lady Chilton, and had satisfied myself that the cries had not come from your daughter, I left your wife's room as soon as I could. Of course you are free to have words with my superior if you still consider my conduct to have been a breach of etiquette. That is your prerogative,' said Ravenscroft seeking to placate his accuser.

'Yes, yes,' interrupted Chilton in an irritable tone of voice. 'I would be obliged, sir, in the future, if you would kindly ask my permission before you speak to my wife again.'

'Of course sir,' replied Ravenscroft, grateful that the other's anger had subsided.

'I hear you have been to see Russell. Why?'

'Yes sir, because I understand that you and Mr Russell have had a recent falling out,' said Ravenscroft, noting Brockway's unease in the corner of the room.

'The man is a time waster and philanderer,' stated Chilton.

'I believe that you wished to purchase some land from Mr Russell, but that he was not inclined to sell?'

'Wanted too much for it. I told him I was buying the land because I believed there was salt beneath it, not gold. You think Russell has my daughter?'

'I have no evidence to suggest that is the case.'

'You searched his buildings?'

'No sir.'

'Well don't you think you should have?' demanded Chilton, staring hard at Ravenscroft.

'As I said sir, I have no cause to think that Mr Russell has taken your daughter,' said Ravenscroft, wishing that his interview with Sir Charles would come to a swift conclusion.

'Would have thought a search was imperative.'

'I do not believe that Mr Russell has your daughter.'

'Suppose you know what you are doing,' grumbled Chilton looking down at his papers.

'I will keep you fully informed, sir,' said Ravenscroft.

'Yes, yes.'

'Oh, one more thing, Sir Charles. How did you come to employ Miss Petterson, your daughter's governess?'

'Miss Petterson?'

'Yes sir, did she come recommended to you?'

'I don't know. My wife deals with all that kind of thing.'

'And have you been pleased with Miss Petterson's conduct?' asked Ravenscroft.

'Look, I don't know where all this is leading Ravenscroft. My wife and I have had no cause for complaint against Miss Petterson, and Mildred I believe is quite fond of her. Don't see that any of this has any relevance. I suggest that you get on and find my daughter, Ravenscroft. Now I have business to attend to.'

Ravenscroft and Crabb made a hasty exit from the study, closing the door after them.

'Prickly character,' muttered Crabb.

'Yes indeed. He certainly did not approve of my questioning his wife. I wonder whether her condition has something to do with his overbearing manner? Don't you also find it strange that when we arrived here this afternoon, we were kept waiting for a full ten minutes before Brockway admitted us to the study? If it had been my child who had been abducted in such a fashion I would have wanted to hear the latest news as soon as possible, yet it appears that Sir Charles is more interested in his business affairs than the recovery of his own child.'

'What next sir?' asked Crabb.

'We need to speak to the governess again; I feel that she may be the solution to this mystery.'

'Where might she be?' asked Crabb.

'We could try the schoolroom. I believe it is located on the top floor.'

The two men made their way up the winding staircase onto the main landing, and then climbed the narrower wooden stairs that lead to the upper reaches of the house. Here Ravenscroft knocked on the door of one of the rooms, and was rewarded by a voice he recognized.

'Good day to you, Miss Petterson,' said Ravenscroft entering the schoolroom.

'You have news of Mildred?' asked the governess rising quickly from her school desk and coming forwards to meet the two policemen.

'I am afraid we have little to report, Miss Petterson.'

'I see,' replied the woman turning away.

'We have made thorough searches of the area around Vines Lane, so we can only conclude that whoever took your charge must have left the town,' said Ravenscroft.

'Then we may never find her,' added the governess sadly.

'I hope that we will find her eventually, although that of course may depend on certain people assisting us in our enquiries, and being truthful in their answers,' emphasized Ravenscroft.

'I have told you all that I know.'

'Forgive me, Miss Petterson, if I say that I do not believe that you have been telling us the truth. May we sit down?' asked Ravenscroft observing that the governess's face had become flushed.

'Yes, of course.'

'Now Miss Petterson,' said Ravenscroft seating himself on one of the chairs, 'Do you still maintain that you entered the church with the aim of discovering which hymns had been selected for next Sunday's service?'

'That is what I said, Inspector. I have no cause to say otherwise.'

'It may interest you to know, Miss Petterson, that we have learnt that the vicar has not yet chosen next Sunday's hymns,' said Ravenscroft looking intently at the governess over the top of his spectacles.

'Yes . . . but I did not know that at the time I went into the church. It is the usual practice to change the hymns on a Tuesday.'

'Begging your pardon miss, but you did not say that when we questioned you yesterday,' interjected Crabb.

'I forgot. Of course I went into the church to see what the hymns were, and when I realized that they had not been changed, then I came away.'

'This could not have taken more than a few seconds Miss Petterson, and yet you claimed that you were inside the church for a full five minutes,' said Ravenscroft noticing the woman's unease as she gripped the handkerchief that lay in her lap.

'Perhaps it was less. I am not sure. No, I remember now. Some of the hymn books were spread untidily over the pews. Yes, I picked up the books and returned them to the side-table; I like things to be neat and tidy, and in their proper place. That is what took the time. I am sorry if I have not made myself entirely clear on this matter. Since poor Mildred has disappeared, my mind has been very unsettled. You must forgive my lack of clarity.'

Ravenscroft smiled to himself. 'Miss Petterson, did you meet anyone inside the church?'

'No. I would have said if I had. There was no one else there.'

'You did not arrange to meet anyone in the church?' asked Ravenscroft realizing that the governess had been put on her guard.

'No, of course not.'

'I would like to turn now to another matter. When we talked with you yesterday, you mentioned that you had been previously employed in the household of Lord and Lady Roberts of Warminster.'

'That is correct.'

'It may interest you to know, Miss Petterson, that we have made enquiries in Warmister, and that today we received a reply by telegram to these which states quite clearly that Miss Petterson the governess died in Warminster five years ago. How do you explain that?' asked Ravenscroft confronting the governess and observing her closely.

'I . . . er . . . there must be some mistake?'

'There is no mistake, I can assure you. I have the telegram here.'

'I cannot understand . . . I was employed by Lord and Lady Roberts,' protested the governess.

'Then you would have no objection to accompanying us on an excursion to Warminster. I am sure that Lord and Lady Roberts will be able to confirm or deny your story,' said Ravenscroft beginning to rise up from his chair. 'Shall we go now, Miss Petterson?'

'All right, I will tell you everything,' said the governess anxiously.

'I wish you would, Miss Petterson. The truth would save us all a great deal of time,' said Ravenscroft leaning back in his chair.

'Dear me, this is so difficult. I do not quite know where to begin. Miss Petterson was my sister, Margaret. It was she who was employed by Lord and Lady Roberts in the capacity of governess. I also worked in the house as a ladies maid. My sister died as the result of catching an infection which lead to a fever. It was so unexpected. One day shortly afterwards I saw an advertisement in *The Times*, asking for a governess here at Hill Court. I had in my possession all my sister's past references, and decided to apply for the position: I professed to be my sister seeking a new position. That is how I came to be here,' replied the governess looking down at her hands, as she continued to turn the handkerchief nervously in her lap.

'I see,' replied Ravenscroft. 'Forgive me, Miss Petterson, but surely Sir Charles and Lady Chilton would have also requested references from your sister's employer?'

'Yes of course they did. I intercepted the request and wrote back pretending to be Lady Roberts. It was a shameful thing to have done! I realize that now, but all I wanted to do was to better myself. I did not want to remain a lady's maid for the rest of my life. As my sister was dead, I saw no harm in using her references,' implored the governess, looking into Ravenscroft's eyes.

'Deception to obtain a position in a respectable household is a criminal offence, Miss Petterson,' replied Ravenscroft sternly.

'I know. I realize I have been extremely foolish, but I meant no harm by it, I can assure you. Have you never wanted to improve your standing in society? No one has been harmed by my actions, you must acknowledge that fact, Mr Ravenscroft?'

'Miss Chilton, your charge is still missing.'

'And I had nothing to do with that. I have told you the truth about Mildred's disappearance. If I knew where she was, don't you think I would have told you by now? If only I had not entered the church on that afternoon, then none of this would have happened. I suppose you are now going to inform Sir Charles and Lady Chilton of my deception? Is there anything I can say in my defence?'

'You are not in a court of law, Miss Petterson. I know that your employer speaks well of you, and I understand that Miss Chilton is fond of you, but that does not excuse your previous conduct in this matter.'

'Please, I implore you not to tell Sir Charles. I could not bear that. I have done no harm, Inspector,' pleaded the governess.

'I am prepared to keep this conversation confidential for the moment, Miss Petterson, or at least until Mildred has been returned, but I cannot promise you that this matter can be totally overlooked,' said Ravenscroft rising from his seat.

'Thank you, Inspector.'

'Oh one more thing, Miss Petterson, I wonder if you could identify this handkerchief for us,' said Ravenscroft removing the item from his pocket, and passing it over to the governess.

'Yes, it is Mildred's. There is the letter "M" that I embroidered on it. Where did you find it?' asked the governess with a look of alarm.

'One of my men recovered it from the canal this morning.'

'Oh my God! No!' cried out the governess.

'Do not distress yourself, Miss Petterson. Nobody has been recovered from the canal. Can you confirm that Miss Chilton was in possession of this handkerchief on the day she disappeared?'

'Yes, yes. I am sure.'

'Then it seems highly likely that your charge was taken from the churchyard, by a person or persons unknown, along the path that leads down the hill, and across the railway line, to the side of the canal, and that the handkerchief was dropped there,' said Ravenscroft.

'All this is quite terrible, Inspector.'

'If I may have the handkerchief back? Thank you, Miss Petterson. If you will excuse us, we must both continue with our investigations.'

* * *

A few minutes later Ravenscroft and Crabb stood once more in the churchyard of St. Augustine's church.

'A fine view from up here, Crabb,' said Ravenscroft looking out beyond the canal and river and the salt workings below them, towards the buildings of the town in the distance. 'Now that Miss Petterson has identified the handkerchief, I think we know which way young Mildred was taken.'

'Do you think she was taken aboard a canal barge?' asked Crabb.

'Almost certainly, I would say. That would explain why no one in the area saw the girl and her captor. If Mildred, and the person or persons who took her left the town that way, they would have followed a route which joined the Worcester–Birmingham canal after a few miles, and from there they could have gone either north or south. We must make enquiries of the lock keepers along the canal to see whether they have noticed anything untoward. Unfortunately it is now getting dark, so we must wait for the morning.'

'Do you believe Miss Petterson was telling us the truth? She could have arranged the abduction of the child herself and planted the handkerchief in the canal where it was sure to be found,' suggested Crabb.

'You could well be right, Tom, but I cannot see why she would have arranged such an abduction; she has nothing to gain by such an action — in fact quite the reverse.'

'I don't see sir.'

'Well, she would have known that police enquiries would be made, and that such enquiries might have reveal the truth concerning her deception to secure an appointment here.'

'She lied to us about her time in the church — tidying up the hymn books and such like.'

'Yes. Just why did she go into the church? All this nonsense about finding which hymns had been chosen, and untidy books, I don't believe her for one minute. No, I think she had arranged to meet someone there, although of course she denied that. Furthermore I believe she was inside the church for more than five minutes, giving ample time for Mildred to be taken. I wonder who she met there? Sir Charles, perhaps?'

'Why Sir Charles?' asked Crabb. 'He is her employer.'

'She could have been having a liaison with Chilton. She would not be the first governess to be taken advantage of by her employer.'

'She is a bit too plain if you ask me, and he would probably frighten most women off with his bluff manner if he made advances towards them,' joked Crabb.

'You're probably right Crabb, but we must retain an open mind. A meeting inside the church would have been well away from the house where the servants might have talked. Certainly Sir Charles does not appear to have any feelings towards his wife, so he may have transferred his affections to the governess, but until we have any evidence that Miss Petterson met either her employer, or indeed someone else, in the church, then we cannot accuse her of lying on that account.'

'I suppose you're right sir.'

'What's that, Tom?,' said Ravenscroft suddenly.

'It's that laughing noise again, the same as last night,' replied Crabb.

'Yes, quick — where is it coming from?'

'Over there sir, behind that tree,' indicated Crabb.

'Quickly Tom. Come out man, show yourself!' shouted Ravenscroft as he and Crabb ran forwards.

A figure darted quickly from one side of the tree to behind one of the larger upright stones in the churchyard.

'That's him sir,' said Crabb pointing to the ragged grey-haired man. 'I swear that was the old fellow I chased down the path last night.'

'Can't catch Old John!' laughed the man.

'We would like a word with you, my man. We mean you no harm,' said Ravenscroft walking slowly towards the stone.

'Old John is too quick for thee!' taunted the man, pulling an ugly face as he moved swiftly across to another stone.

'Stop where you are,' commanded Crabb. 'It's the law.'

'Don't like peelers. Can't catch me! Can't catch Old John!'

The man moved swiftly away from the approaching detectives, flinging his arms in the air and laughing as he did so.

'We only want to ask you some questions about the girl who disappeared,' called out Ravenscroft. 'You are not in any trouble. There is nothing to fear.'

'Can't catch Old John!'

'Did you see anything? Did you see who took her?' asked Ravenscroft trying to keep up with the movements of the strange figure.

'Can't catch Old John!' taunted the man.

'For goodness sake stop still!' commanded a frustrated Ravenscroft.

Suddenly the man came to an abrupt halt before a large vault in the corner of the churchyard, before issuing a loud piercing scream. 'No, you shan't have Old John! You can't have me as well!' he cried.

'Good God,' called out Ravenscroft, taken aback by the man's fear. 'Whatever ails you man?'

'You can't have me! He's come back for me! Come back for me!' repeated the man pointing at the tomb.

'See if you can get round the other side of him, Tom,' instructed Ravenscroft as they moved nearer the figure.

'He has come back for me! Master has come back for me. Yer not taking Old John!' shouted the man briefly turning in the detectives' direction, before laughing out loud once more, and darting quickly from the churchyard. 'Can't catch Old John!'

'Shall I get after him sir?' asked Crabb, as the figure disappeared from view.

'I fear he will be too quick for us again, Tom. Let him go.'

'Strange fellow. How old do you think he was, sir?'

'Difficult to tell by his dirty bedraggled appearance. Certainly many years older than you or me.'

'Fellow was half-soaked if you ask me.'

'Did you notice how he stopped suddenly by that vault and let out that loud scream? You would have thought that he had seen a ghost of some sort. How odd! We'll make enquiries in the town tomorrow and see what people can tell us about him.'

'Don't expect he can help us anyway,' added Crabb.

'I'm inclined to agree with you. If the man did see the girl being abducted, I doubt whether he would have any sense at all to describe the event to us. Come Tom, the night is drawing in. We can't do any more today; let us return home.'

CHAPTER SIX

LEDBURY

'Well my dear it seems that we are both faced with mysteries that may prove difficult to solve.'

Ravenscroft was sitting with his wife, later that evening, before a roaring fire in their small house in Church Lane.

'But what am I to tell poor Miss Corbett?' asked Lucy.

'I think it was very bold of you to take yourself off to Cheltenham like that,' replied Ravenscroft seeking to evade the question.

'I could do little else. If you had seen how distressed she was, in this very room, you would also have felt compelled to do all within your power to reunite her with her poor infant child.'

'I am sure there must be some logical explanation for all this,' said Ravenscroft, placing another log on the fire whilst attempting to lighten his wife's anxiety.

'That is what I thought, but you have seen the letter. Twenty-two Suffolk Square, Montpelier, Cheltenham. Mrs Amelia Huddlestone. There is no other address it could be, and no one in the area has heard of the Huddlestones.'

'Then I think we must conclude that the woman Huddlestone gave a false name and address.'

'But why, Samuel? Why would she do that? I do not understand what she could gain by such deception.'

'You say that, according to Miss Corbett, this woman Huddlestone had just lost her own child and that that was the reason for her anxiety, and for her desire to look after the infant Lily. If that is the case, she may have given the false address and gone elsewhere in case the mother should later reappear and want her child back. I can see how such a demand would cause problems for both the child, and for her new guardians.'

'Then we have no chance of finding the Huddlestones,' said a dispirited Lucy staring into the fire. 'There is nothing more that I can do.'

'There is one disturbing fact about this case — you say that Miss Corbett gave the woman £5 when she handed over the child?'

'Yes — apparently it was agreed that the £5 would go some way towards the initial expenses the Huddlestones would incur. Oh no! You don't think the woman took the money and then abandoned the child!' cried out Lucy.

'Unfortunately that may well be the case. Certainly in Whitechapel I would often come across poor unfortunates who were often more than prepared to give their children away, to what they perceived as a good home, in order to relieve themselves of their own personal responsibilities — and there were certainly other unscrupulous characters who were more than willing to take advantage of such orphan children.'

'But that is terrible,' said Lucy becoming more agitated. 'To think that poor Lily has been given away to that terrible Huddlestone woman. She may be dying of hunger as we speak, or even be dead!'

'There, there, my dear, I am sure that is not the case. It may all be a misunderstanding and everything will come right in the end. We may yet discover the whereabouts of this Mrs Huddlestone and you will then be able to reunite mother and child,' said Ravenscroft placing a reassuring hand on his wife's shoulder.

'How on earth am I going to do that, when the Huddlestones are nowhere to be found in Cheltenham?'

'We must look further afield. The letter itself does not appear to offer us any clues. How did your Miss Corbett learn of this Mrs Huddlestone?'

'She replied to an advertisement in a local newspaper.'

'Did she tell you the name of the newspaper?'

'Apparently she was living on a farm in Hanbury at the time, and saw the advertisement in a Droitwich newspaper. I think it was the Droitwich News or something like that — no, The Droitwich Advertiser, I'm sure that was the name of the publication,' said Lucy optimistically.

'There we have it! A visit to the offices of The Droitwich Advertiser might discover the true name and address of the person who placed the advertisement, or at least may provide us with the names of similar unfortunate women who may have responded to Mrs Huddlestone request.'

'Samuel, you are wonderful,' said Lucy leaning over and kissing her husband, 'I knew you would think of a solution. I shall travel with you to Droitwich tomorrow and visit the newspaper office in person.'

'Do you think that is wise, my dear?' asked Ravenscroft. 'We do not know where all this is going to lead. It was very brave of you to have undertaken the journey to Cheltenham today.'

'Well you are too busy to investigate this case at the present, and what harm can befall me in making enquiries at a newspaper office?'

'Lucy, I am very proud of your actions in support of your Miss Corbett, and I know that you, more than most people, are entirely sympathetic to her situation. To give away your only child is a crime against nature, that would haunt one for the rest of one's days. Of course you shall go, but only upon one condition.'

'Yes, Samuel?'

'If you are fortunate enough to discover either the true identity of this mysterious Huddlestone woman, or to find out the names of other unfortunate women, you will not act upon any of that information until you have consulted me.'

'Of course, but whatever for?'

'This Mrs Huddlestone may be a dangerous woman.'

'We don't know that yet,' interrupted Lucy.

'No we do not, and as I said, there may be a perfectly innocent explanation for all of this — but until we are in receipt of all the facts, we must err on the side of caution. Promise me that you will not do anything foolish.'

'Oh Samuel, I'm sure you are exaggerating the danger.'

'Promise me?' said Ravenscroft leaning forwards and taking his wife's hand within his own. 'I came close to losing you in that cottage up on the hills, I could not bear to go through such torture again.'

'Dear Samuel, I promise that I will not do anything foolish,' replied a smiling Lucy. 'Now tell me more about your case. It sounds perfectly dreadful that someone should have taken that poor girl. Whatever for?'

'I wish I knew that, my dear. At present I can find no reason at all why anyone would have wanted to take the girl. Sir Charles Chilton is not particularly well liked by the town's people, but the family have received no threats in the past, and no demands for money have been made since the girl was taken,' sighed Ravenscroft.

'From what you have told me, that governess has a lot to answer for. Fancy leaving the child to play alone in the churchyard, whilst she went inside the church. I think you should question her more. She does not sound like a woman to be trusted,' suggested Lucy.

'You are probably right, but I can see no reason why she would have been involved in the girl's abduction. She has nothing to gain by it. No, I think whoever took the girl placed her on one of the salt barges and made their escape that way. All we can do now is to see whether we can trace their route along the canal, and hope that the lock keepers, or the canal folk, may have seen something.'

'Let us hope you are successful. It is strange that you are looking for a young girl who has been cruelly abducted from her family, and that I am trying to reunite a young infant with her natural mother. And both have connections with Droitwich. Miss Corbett gave her baby away at the station in Droitwich, and your Miss Chilton was taken from Dodderhill church just outside Droitwich. Rather a coincidence, don't you consider? You don't think the two events are connected in some way?' asked Lucy.

'At the moment I cannot see how they are. We don't know that your Miss Corbett's baby has been taken against her mother's will; there may yet be a simple explanation as to why you could not find the Huddlestones — I am sure you will discover the truth tomorrow. Several months seem to separate the two events.

'It is late my dear, and both of us will have an early start in the morning. Let us hope that Tom and I will soon find out who has taken the Chilton girl, and that we will be able to bring her home safely, to her parents.'

CHAPTER SEVEN

DROITWICH

Lucy looked intently at the worn brass plate that was attached to the oak door of the old black and white three-storey building. She was standing on the main street of Droitwich; she peered closely and eventually made out the letters Droitwich Advertiser. Confident that she had found the correct address, she pushed open the door, and gradually made her way up the dimly lit flight of creaking steps.

After knocking twice, and receiving no answer, she decided to push open the door. As she entered the room, a large marmalade coloured cat gave out a loud squawk of annoyance as it brushed quickly past her legs and out onto the landing.

'Good day. Is anyone there?' Lucy called as she looked at the rows of ancient ledgers that graced every wall of the room, and the piles of untidy books and papers that littered a large desk and the floor. A thin shaft of sunlight stretched across a thread-bare patterned carpet, highlighting a brown-stained, chipped teacup and saucer which lay on a box of typeface letters.

'Sorry, we don't accept advertisements on Thursdays. You are too late for this week's issue anyway,' said a short, grey-haired man entering from an inner room.

'I have not come to place an advertisement, but to make an enquiry,' replied Lucy hesitantly.

'Then you will have to go to the library, that's where all the back copies are kept,' muttered the man turning away, and searching through one of the stacks of papers on his desk.

'I was rather hoping you would be able to help me.'

'Sorry, madam, cannot help you today. Paper has to be printed. Readers to be reached. Advertisers to be pleased. No time to spare. Now where did I put that article on brine,' said the man speaking in short sharp sentences.

'Brine?' enquired Lucy.

'Salt, my dear lady, salt. The fortunes of Droitwich are based on salt. No salt; no Droitwich. I really must find that article — ah, here we are,' replied the man holding up the missing sheet of paper with a degree of triumph, before turning on his heel and making his way back into his inner sanctum.

'If you could but spare me a moment of your precious time sir, I would be most obliged,' called out Lucy, wondering whether her journey might have been in vain.

'Time! Time! Time, my dear lady, is something which idle people seek to expand, whereas those of us who are fully engaged attempt to harness,' uttered the newspaper man with a degree of indignation, as he disappeared from view.

'It is a police matter, sir.'

A moment's silence ensued before a face peered round the corner of the inner door. 'Police matter, you say. Since when have the police employed gentle ladies to conduct their business?'

'I am not actually a member of the police force. It is my husband—'

'Your husband! Then why is he not here to ask the questions?' demanded the other indignantly.

'He is busy on a case at the moment. A local girl has gone missing.'

'Really. A local girl gone missing you say!' exclaimed the newspaper man returning quickly to the main room. 'Why on earth did you not mention that before. A missing person indeed! And your husband is leading the enquiry. May I be so bold as to make enquiries regarding the name of your husband, ma'am?'

'Ravenscroft. Detective Inspector Ravenscroft.'

'Ravenscroft you say. Now where have I heard that name before? Ravenscroft? Ravenscroft? Ravenscroft? Ah yes, I have it. Worcester. Cathedral. Lost book. Missing librarian. A year or so ago. Nasty business if I recall. Well my dear lady, a missing girl you say? That changes everything. Indeed. Do please take a seat. You must tell me all about it,' said the man vigorously brushing away a gathering of papers that littered the seat of an old wooden chair.

'Thank you,' said Lucy encouraged by the other's interest.

'Now if you would kindly pause a moment, Mrs Ravenscroft, whilst I secure pen and paper. The name is Shorter. Clement Shorter. Editor, reporter, printer, advertising manager, and proprietor of the Droitwich Advertiser at your service,' said the newspaperman wiping an ink stained hand on his leather apron, before extending it in Lucy's direction. 'I am very pleased to make your acquaintance, ma'am.'

'And I yours, Mister Shorter,' replied a relieved Lucy, as her hand was vigorously shaken by the newspaperman.

'Disappearing girl you say? In Droitwich? Surprised I have not been informed before. Local story you say? Not much happens in Droitwich of a dramatic nature. This will interest our readers greatly. If we are very quick and industrious, I am sure we could include it in this week's issue. That gardening item wasn't of a particular interest anyway. It will not be missed. Never been able to understand why people are so interested in their gardens. If one is fully occupied, there is no time for a garden, I say. Cannot see the point in them. You have a garden, Mrs Ravenscroft? No? Very sensible. Gardens — a complete waste of time and effort. Alas, hardly a month goes by in the spring and summer when I can avoid a visit to some dreary flower show or other. I would avoid it if I could, but people expect it of one. Improves the sales of the newspaper if they purchase that week's copy in order to see their name in print — "Mr Jones was the winner of the prize marrow category; Mrs Brown's floral display exceeded all expectations". Mundane to say the least,' sighed Shorter returning to his desk.

'Mr Shorter, it is not my husband's case that has bought me here today,' interrupted Lucy.

'Oh my dear Mrs Ravenscroft, I hope you are not going to disappoint me? It has been such a long time since the Droitwich Advertiser has been able to report anything of great criminal interest. Ah here we are!' exclaimed the news-paper man suddenly holding a pen and paper up high. 'That which is lost has been found! The errant sheep returns to the fold, as they say.'

'I'm afraid I cannot tell you anything about the disap-pearance, because I know very little about it. As I said, my husband is occupied in investigating the case, and I have come here today on an entirely different errand,' said Lucy anxious to turn the conversation away from her husband's activities.

'I see. What a pity,' muttered Shorter looking somewhat crestfallen as he fell back into his seat. 'Another hope dashed! Another avenue closed! Such a promising expectation now demoted to the file labelled "great stories that might have been". That is a shame, my dear Mrs Ravenscroft, a great shame.'

'It is a matter of some importance concerning an adver-tisement that was placed in your paper some months ago,' said Lucy trying to sound encouraging. 'The advertisement was placed by a lady of the name Huddlestone, who was seeking to adopt a young infant to bring up as her own.'

'Advertisement you say? This enquiry of yours is of a police nature?' asked the newspaper editor, raising his eye-brows as he leaned forwards in his seat.

'It may well turn out to be a police matter, Mr Shorter.'

'Well you should have said earlier! Police matter you say. Perhaps one's expectations are not dashed after all.

Advertisement placed by one Huddlestone,' said Shorter rising enthusiastically from his chair. 'Seeking child to acquire as her own, you say. Placed a few months ago. Could you perhaps be more precise as to the date, Mrs Ravenscroft?'

'I believe the advertisement may have been placed around October of last year.'

'Last October you say. Let me see,' said Shorter striding over to a nearby bookcase and energetically turning over a large pile of newspapers. 'Yes, here we are. This file should contain last autumn's papers. We should be able to find what you are looking for.'

'Can I be of any assistance?' asked Lucy.

'Nothing to concern you, my dear lady,' replied the editor brushing aside a pile of papers and books on his desk, before banging down the file of newspapers on to the dusty surface. 'Advertisement in the name of Huddlestone. Now where are my glasses? Eyes not so good as they once were. Always losing them. Must be here somewhere. Confound it! Perhaps I left them in the other room?'

'I believe your spectacles are to be found on top of your head Mr Shorter,' said Lucy trying to sound helpful.

'My head?' said Shorter looking perplexed.

'Your spectacles, on top of your head,' repeated Lucy pointing.

'Head? Yes of course. How silly of me. Must have placed them there earlier. Such a nuisance, but an essential nuisance I grant you. Now let me see. First week in October. Anything there?' said the editor replacing the glasses on the end of his nose, before turning over the first few pages of the issue on top of the pile, and running his finger down one of the pages. 'Man seeking lost dog. Women's Christian Association Monthly Meeting, Liver Pills. Droitwich Temperance. Mundane all of it! Mundane! No, nothing there I'm afraid. Let us try the following week. I am sure we will find it there somewhere. Huddlestone you say? Ah, here we are. "Lady mourning for the sudden loss of her own infant child, offers good home and upbringing for unwanted child.

Name of Huddlestone." How very sad, very sad, and how very Christian. Therein lies a story, no doubt.'

'Does the advertisement give an address, or any further details?' asked Lucy rising from her seat and crossing over eagerly to where the newspaper man stood.

'Box Number!' pronounced Shorter.

'Box Number. What does that mean?'

'It means that anyone who wishes to reply to the advertisement should write a letter to the box number stated, care of this newspaper.'

'And what would happen next?'

'Well, we usually wait a few days, to see if there are a number of replies, then we forward them all on to the person who placed the advertisement, and that is the end of the matter as far as we are concerned. It is then up to the advertiser and those who have replied to correspond with one another, should they so wish.'

'It seems rather a long drawn-out process,' said Lucy. 'Why shouldn't advertisers give their own addresses in the first place?'

'Privacy. Privacy, my dear Mrs Ravenscroft. Some of our readers and advertisers wish to conduct their affairs in a discreet and personal manner. Why, to give one's own address in the public domain, is to open one not only to social ridicule, but also to every kind of theft and skulduggery. Believe me my dear lady when I tell you that the world is full of those who are more than anxious to take advantage of another's good intentions,' pronounced Shorter shaking his head.

'I see. Tell me Mr Shorter, do you still have the address of the person who placed this advertisement,' asked Lucy hopefully.

'Highly unlikely — but not impossible,' replied Shorter peering over the top of his spectacles in Lucy's direction.

'How do you mean?'

'Well, we usually retain advertisers' addresses for a few weeks or so, so that we can forward the replies onto them

— then I'm afraid we usually discard them, that is if we are fortunate enough to find them again.'

'You say "we". I was given to understand that the enterprise was entirely your own?'

'Why, yes indeed. I use the term 'we' out of professional familiarity. It sounds so much better to suggest that there are more than one of us — but alas there is only my poor presence here to keep the fires of the free press in Droitwich burning brightly in this world of darkened skies of mediocrity and ignorance,' replied Shorter looking downcast.

'I am sorry for it,' said Lucy sympathetically. 'You must find your work arduous and lonely?'

'At times, my dear lady, but then there are always people calling upon one with snippets of news which they consider may be of interest to our readers, people placing advertisements, people like yourself making enquiries, people wanting you to attend their meetings or flower shows, people wanting to provide interviews. In fact, when I come to think of it, there is never a dull moment. There is always the paper to be produced, once every week. Time, as I said earlier my dear Mrs Ravenscroft, can be the enemy, always seeking to undermine one with its relentless march ever onwards, unless of course it can be mastered to one's personal will. No, one is never lonely. There is always Clarence for company.'

'Clarence?' asked Lucy intrigued.

'Clarence. You may well have encountered him on the stairs as you came in.'

'Oh, yes, the cat.'

'Clarence, such a good example of the frustrating feline fraternity — indifferent to one's feelings one minute, inspirational the next. You have a cat, Mrs Ravenscroft? No I think not. Such contradictory creatures. Useful for preserving the papers from the ravages of the mice — such spiritual creatures, but Clarence can be quite unsettling at other times.'

'Do you think it may be possible for you to find the address of the advertiser?' asked Lucy anxious to steer the conversation back to the matter in hand.

'Who knows, Mrs Ravenscroft, who knows?' replied Shorter throwing his arms wide. 'Pray look around you ma'am. Somewhere in this room there may be a scrap of small paper which may provide us with the information you are looking for — but where to begin? Where to begin? Here you see around you the accumulated knowledge of the last twenty years of the Droitwich Advertiser. You see my dilemma?'

'I do indeed,' said Lucy sighing.

'Somewhere in the dark recesses of this room, hidden between a thousand sheets of ancient newsprint may be the precious item which we seek. But then, of course, it may not be there at all. Cast out into the wilderness weeks ago with items of a similar disposition. All I can offer you is the distant hope that the item under discussion may present itself when one is least expecting it. That is all I can say.'

'I see,' said Lucy looking downcast, realizing that her mission was facing failure.

'If you would care to leave me your address, I will certainly forward the information onto you, should it come to light.'

'Thank you.'

'If you would be so kind as to write on this piece of paper.'

Lucy took the pen and wrote out her name and address, but without any degree of conviction, knowing that in all probability her piece of paper would befall the same fate as the Huddlestone item.

'Thank you, Mrs Ravenscroft. Never fear, I shall safeguard your information with the utmost care, and will contact you the moment the missing item comes to life.'

'Tell me, Mr Shorter. I don't suppose you happen to know how many people replied to the advertisement?'

'Ah, I do indeed. Two — to be precise!'

'How do you know that?' asked Lucy startled by this sudden disclosure.

'See here,' said Shorter proudly pointing to the advertisement in the newspaper. 'See those pencil marks. We — I

— always make a record by the side of an advertisement when it receives a reply. Two marks mean two people replied.'

'I'm impressed,' said Lucy smiling. 'I wonder if it would be possible for you to tell me the names of those two people?'

'Ah, now you are asking a very difficult question.'

'I am sorry.'

'Two replies,' muttered Shorter casting his eyes upwards at the ceiling of the room.

Lucy stood in silence, not wishing the disturb the editor's thoughts.

'Two replies. Unfortunately I cannot help you, alas. I believe the replies were enclosed within envelopes to be forwarded, with the box number and address of the newspaper written on the outer envelope.'

'I see,' said Lucy trying not to sound too disappointed. 'Thank you, Mr Shorter, you have been most helpful. If you are able to find the address of Mrs Huddlestone then I would be most grateful if you would contact me. There is a distressed mother waiting for news of the child she unfortunately gave away. Anyway, I will not take up any more of your precious time.'

'Gave away her baby you say. Gave away her baby. Where have I read those words before. Yes of course! One moment, please, Mrs Ravenscroft,' said Shorter eagerly turning over a few copies of the newspaper.

Lucy came nearer, wondering what item of information was about to be revealed by the newspaper man.

'Yes, yes, I have it. Local girl commits suicide!' said Shorter reading from a page. 'Distressed state of mind, after loss of her only child!'

'Good heavens, how terrible!' exclaimed Lucy.

'"The inquest was held at The Raven Inn, last Wednesday morning, concerning the apparent suicide of one Belinda Parkes, age 18, formerly employed as a housemaid at Hill Court, Dodderhill, Droitwich. George Richardson, a local bargeman, stated that he had discovered the body of a young woman in the canal near Crutch Lane, the previous Thursday morning. He pulled the body from the waterway and was able to identify the young woman as Belinda Parkes, as both he and the deceased had been former members of the congregation of Dodderhill Church. Mrs Greenway, cook at Hill Court, stated that the deceased woman had been of unsettled mind for the past week or more. Apparently she had given birth to an illegitimate child three months previously, but shortly after its birth had given up the child for adoption. She had become anxious regarding the welfare of her infant, and had become increasingly distressed when she had been unable to visit her child. The Coroner recorded a verdict of death by suicide."'

'How awful!' said Lucy turning away, bringing a hand towards her face, and seeking to control the tears of sadness that began to form in her eyes.

'My dear Mrs Ravenscroft, please do accept a chair. I would not have read this article out loud, had I considered that it would in any way distress you. I hope you are not related in any way to the deceased?'

'No, not at all. It is just that another young lady, of similar misfortune, visited me yesterday, and recounted how she had replied to the advertisement in your newspaper — and how she had given away her only child to this Mrs Huddlestone,' said Lucy blurting out the words.

'I see, how sad,' sympathized Shorter.

'And when she sought to visit her child, she discovered that both the woman and child were not living at the address she had been given.'

'Dear me,' said Shorter shaking his head. 'It would seem that this Belinda Parkes had also replied to the same advertisement, and that the same misfortune had clearly befallen her.'

'Mr Shorter, if you will excuse me. Thank you once again for your assistance,' said Lucy forcing back the tears as she walked quickly out of the room.

'My dear Mrs Ravenscroft, please stay until—' began Shorter, but his visitor had already made her way down the long flight of steps, and had disappeared from view.

CHAPTER EIGHT

DROITWICH

'Well, Tom. Have we any news?'

It was later that same day, and Ravenscroft and Crabb met once again outside the church of St. Augustine at Dodderhill.

'Nothing sir. None of the lock keepers report anything unusual. Just the usual barges going up and down the canal with their cargoes,' replied Crabb.

'How far is it until the Droitwich canal joins the Worcester–Birmingham canal?'

'No more than two or three miles until you get to Hanbury Wharf, I believe. After that the boats either turn north to Stoke Works and Tardebigge on their way to Birmingham, or south towards Worcester.'

'So whoever abducted Miss Chilton could be any-where with her by now. What I don't understand is why anyone would have taken her in the first place. The fam-ily have received no calls for money for her return,' replied Ravenscroft deep in thought.

'It is certainly a strange case, sir,' added Crabb.

'Yes, and since your departure Tom, the case has taken a new direction. I believe I mentioned to you that Mrs

Ravenscroft was attempting to discover what had happened to a young child which had been given away by her mother. Well, today she visited the local newspaper office here in the town, where she learnt that a few months ago a young housemaid by the name of Belinda Parkes had likewise given her baby away in reply to an advertisement.'

'What is the connection to our present case, sir?'

'Nothing, or so I thought, until I learnt that the housemaid came from Hill Court, and furthermore she was so overcome by not being able to recover her baby that she committed suicide.'

'Poor girl,' sympathized Crabb.

'At first I had not thought that all these cases were connected, but now that I have learnt that the maid worked at Hill Court, I am not so sure.'

'What shall we do next then, sir.'

'Let's go and have a word with Mrs Greenway, the cook. Apparently she gave evidence at the girl's inquest.'

* * *

'Ah! If it isn't Mister Ravenscroft again,' said the cook rising from her seat at the table as the two men walked into the kitchens of Hill Court.

'Good day to you Mrs Greenway, and to you Mister Jukes,' said Ravenscroft. 'This is Constable Crabb.'

'Sit yourselves down gentlemen, whilst I makes you a cup of tea,' smiled Mrs Greenway.

'Nothing for me, I thank you,' replied Ravenscroft accepting the chair.

'Your constable looks as though he could do with something to eat. Why don't you try a slice of my home made fruit cake?'

'Thank you. I don't mind if I do,' said Crabb accepting the other chair.

'Have you any news of Miss Mildred?' asked a concerned Jukes.

'I'm afraid not. We have contacted all the stations in the county, and some of my men are making enquiries along the canal path,' replied Ravenscroft.

'The poor mite. Never did any harm to anyone. Now look what has happened to her,' sighed the cook passing over a piece of cake on a plate to Crabb.

'Actually it is another matter that I have come to ask you about Mrs Greenway. What can you tell me about Belinda Parkes? I understand that she was employed here and that you gave evidence at her inquest?' asked Ravenscroft.

'Oh the poor girl. So unfortunate. She was another who had done no harm to anyone. Forced to give away her baby she was.'

'Why was that?'

'Sir Charles, he would not have her in the house unless she got rid of the baby. The poor girl was at a loss, her with a young babby about to be cast out — at her wits end she was. Then she saw the advertisement in the Droitwich Guardian. Nice couple in Cheltenham wanted to adopt a baby. Seemed like a godsend at the time.'

'Tell me Mrs Greenway, do you know whether Belinda gave any money to these people when they took her baby?' asked Ravenscroft becoming more and more interested in the cook's revelations.

'Yes. Five pounds I believe. Belinda had a little money put by, but Jukes and I helped her out.'

'That was very Christian of you both,' said Ravenscroft. 'I don't suppose you know the name of the couple who took the child?'

'Henderson, or something like that, I think,' replied the cook.

'I think it was Huddlestone,' corrected Jukes.

'Huddlestone. Yes, that was it. Huddlestone.'

'And what happened afterwards, after Miss Parkes gave the baby away?'

'Well she pined something terrible for that babby. Regretted it as soon as she had given her away. Full of remorse she was,' sighed the cook.

'Did she try and get the baby back?' asked Crabb his mouth full of cake.

'She tried, but it were no use,' said Jukes.

'She couldn't find where those Huddlestone had gone. Vanished into thin air they had,' said Mrs Greenway. 'She was so distressed. Took her own life. Said there was nothing worth living for now that she had given her babby away, and that the Lord would never forgive her for what she had done. It were a terrible business,' replied the cook, tears beginning to form in her eyes.

'I know this is rather a delicate question, but did Miss Parkes ever confide in you as to the name of the father?' asked Ravenscroft leaning forwards across the table.

'No. She never said.'

'Probably some young lad in the town,' suggested Jukes.

'I don't suppose you have any papers or personal effects belonging to Miss Parkes?'

'Nothing. There were a few letters and such like, but we burnt everything.'

'Thank you Mrs Greenway, you have been most helpful,' said Ravenscroft rising from his seat.

'You don't think any of this has anything to do with Miss Mildred's disappearance?' asked the cook looking perplexed.

'I cannot say at the present. The two events seem unrelated, but we must keep an open mind. Come, Crabb, we have things to do.'

* * *

'Well sir, that does not seem to bring us any more forwards in our investigations,' said Crabb as he and Ravenscroft strode through the kitchen garden.

'No. It merely confirms what Mrs Ravenscroft has told me.'

'I suppose those Huddlestones could have taken Miss Chilton, as well as those babies?'

'I cannot see why they should. The Huddlestones placed an advertisement in the local paper asking for a baby to adopt, pocket the five pounds when they acquire the children, give a false address, and then move on elsewhere no doubt. I fear for the babies they've acquired. It seems highly unlikely they would return to the area to kidnap Miss Chilton. If they had taken Miss Chilton, I feel sure they would undoubtedly have asked for money by now. I believe we are dealing with two different cases here. I think we will have to put the Huddlestones on one side for now, especially as all that happened several months ago, and concentrate on the missing girl.'

'What do we do now sir?'

'I must admit that I am at a loss as to our next move, until we have the results from those telegrams you sent out to the lock keepers. Why don't we go to the Gardeners Arms and see what they can tell us about our friend Old John. By the way, how did you enjoy your cake, Tom?'

'Delicious sir, nearly as good as Mrs Crabb makes.'

'Hm, Queen Anne must have changed the recipe.'

* * *

A few minutes later Ravenscroft and Crabb entered the bar of The Gardeners Arms in Vines Lane.

'Good day to you, gentlemen,' said the burly landlord from the other side of the bar.

'Good morning to you, landlord.'

'You must be Ravenscroft? What can I get you?'

'Two tankards of your finest ale. I believe you know my constable,' replied Ravenscroft.

The landlord nodded in Crabb's direction and began to fill the tankards. Ravenscroft looked round the room with its old wooden tables and chairs, its brown stained walls and the faded photograph of a cricket team above the bar.

'You found that girl yet?' asked the man after a few seconds had elapsed and he had placed the two containers of drink on the counter.

'I'm afraid not. We think she may have been taken on one of the barges.'

'Could be.'

'I don't suppose you know anything about her disappearance?' asked Ravenscroft after sampling the ale.

'Can't help you there, I am afraid. Told your constable I had seen nothing the day that girl disappeared,' replied the landlord leaning on the counter.

'You noticed nothing unusual?'

'That's what I said.'

'No one out of the ordinary who might have called in here on that day? A stranger who had just arrived in the town?' persisted Ravenscroft.

'Only the regulars.'

'What can you tell me about Old John?'

'Old John!' laughed the landlord. 'Old John. Bit simple in the head if you ask me, but he's harmless enough. Why? What's he been doing now?'

'Nothing in particular,' replied Crabb.

'We have encountered him upon two occasions in the churchyard,' added Ravenscroft.

'I'm not surprised. He spends all his time up there. He must be more fond of the dead than the living. Some says he even sleeps on top of the tombs.'

'Has he always been like that?' asked Ravenscroft.

'For as long as I can remember. We give him some of our leftover food, and some folk in the lane give him what they can. Used to work at the big house when he were young, I believe.'

'You mean Hill Court?' asked Ravenscroft.

'So folk says. Before I came here of course. Can I get you gents another one?'

'I think one will suffice, excellent as it is,' replied Ravenscroft draining his tankard. 'What can you tell me about Belinda Parkes?'

'One of the maids at Hill Court?'

Ravenscroft nodded.

'Sad business. Drowned in the canal just over yonder. Bit weak in the head or so they said. Something about a baby, I believe. Gave it away by all accounts. I ask you, what kind of mother gives away her own kind? It ain't natural, is it?'

'No indeed. Did she ever frequent your establishment?' asked Ravenscroft.

'No.'

'Well, thank you for your time.'

'I wish you well with your investigations. The sooner that girl is bought home the better,' said the landlord wiping down the counter.

'You are sure that you saw no one come down the path from the church that afternoon? I ask because your inn is quite near the entrance to the path?' asked Ravenscroft as he and Crabb began to leave the room.

'As I told your constable, I saw no one come down from the church.'

'Thank you. We will take our leave,' said Ravenscroft opening the door.

'I did see someone go up though,' said the landlord turning away.

'You saw someone going up the path?'

'Mr Russell. Seemed in a hurry, he did.'

'Mr Russell you say?'

'That's what I said.'

'Russell. Why on earth didn't you tell this to my constable when he asked you yesterday?' asked an annoyed Ravenscroft.

'Ah well, he didn't ask me who went up the path: only if anyone had come down it, so I said no one. Now if he had asked me—'

'Very well!' sighed Ravenscroft holding his hands up. 'Come on, Crabb, let us go and see Mr Russell.'

* * *

Ravenscroft bought down his fist on the old oak door. 'Mr Russell. Mr Russell, I'd be obliged if you would open the door.'

'Shall I go and look in the barns, sir? He could be holding the girl in one of them.'

'We shall see,' said Ravenscroft banging on the door once more.

'All right, all right. I'm coming,' said Russell opening the door suddenly. 'Oh it's you Ravenscroft; you're making enough noise to wake the dead.'

'I would like further words with you Mr Russell, if I may. May we enter?'

'Not convenient at the moment,' said Russell stepping out of the building and closing the door behind him. 'Say what you have to say out here.'

'You did not tell us, on our previous visit, that you were at Dodderhill church on the day Miss Chilton disappeared,' said Ravenscroft, trying to sound as serious as he could.

'You never asked me. Who says so, anyway?' replied Russell adopting a defensive manner.

'The landlord of The Gardeners Arms. He saw you go up the path in the direction of the church, shortly before Miss Chilton went missing.'

'I suppose I might have gone up that way. What's it to you anyway?'

'It is everything to me Mr Russell, especially when a young girl has been taken against her will. What were you doing in the churchyard?' demanded Ravenscroft observing Russell closely.

'What do people do in churchyards? They visit the graves,' replied Russell caustically.

'Don't waste my time, Mr Russell. What were you doing in the churchyard that afternoon? Did you take the girl?'

'Of course not. I never saw the girl. I was visiting the churchyard to pay my respects to my late mother. She died some twenty years ago and is buried there. I like to take some flowers for her grave, from time to time. There is nothing wrong with that, is there?'

'How long were you there for, in the churchyard?' continued Ravenscroft.

'Ten minutes perhaps.'

'Did you see anyone while you were there?'

'No. No one.'

'Are you sure, Mr Russell?'

'I've told you, Ravenscroft, there was no one there — oh, there was Old John of course.'

'Old John!' exclaimed Crabb.

'Yes, he was sitting on one of the tombs. He's often there.'

'Was he still there when you left?' asked Ravenscroft.

'Yes, I think so.'

'What happened when you left the churchyard?'

'I walked down the path back to the Vines.'

'But the landlord of the Gardeners said he did not see you come down that way,' said Ravenscroft.

'Then he must be mistaken. Oh yes, of course, I took the other path that comes out nearer the bridge.'

'I must say, Mr Russell, I am not entirely happy with your answers.'

'I've told you all I know. You will just have to accept what I say.'

'I must insist that I search your premises,' said Ravenscroft taking a step forward.

'Whatever for, man?'

'I believe you may be holding Miss Chilton against her will.'

'That is ridiculous. Why would I want to take the girl? I have no interest in this matter.'

'If you would permit my constable and myself to enter,' said Ravenscroft moving towards the door.

'The deuce I will!' retorted Russell, moving to bar the detective's way.

'Mr Russell, I must insist that we enter. If you are not holding the girl, then you have nothing to hide,' insisted Ravenscroft. 'If you hinder our progress I will have no alternative but to arrest you and take you into custody.'

'All right, all right man. Stop. Look it's deuce difficult at the moment. Man to man, I'm entertaining a lady — in private, if you get my drift,' said Russell in a quieter tone of voice. 'Discretion and all that.'

'That's as maybe. Step aside Mr Russell, or my constable will take you into custody,' demanded Ravenscroft.

'Confound it,' sighed Russell reluctantly moving to one side.

'Thank you, Mr Russell,' replied Ravenscroft quickly entering the building, closely followed by Crabb.

The policemen found themselves in the large living room of the farmhouse. Ravenscroft looked around at the massive oak table and chairs in the centre of the room and at the old family portraits that adorned the walls.

'I hope you are content now,' said Russell.

'I thought I heard a sound upstairs,' said Ravenscroft running out of the room and ascending the stairs two steps at a time. Flinging open the closed door at the top of the landing, he was confronted by a familiar figure.

'Miss Petterson!' exclaimed Ravenscroft.

'I am so sorry, my dear,' said Russell barging past Crabb at the entrance of the room. 'I tried to stop them, but they insisted. They think we have taken the girl.'

'Miss Petterson, I am surprised to find you here,' said Ravenscroft.

'Don't say anything, Jane. Look Ravenscroft, Miss Petterson has done nothing incorrect. It is just that if her employer, Sir Charles, were to discover our . . . our association he would certainly dismiss Miss Petterson from her post. You know how he hates me,' said Russell stepping over to the governess and placing his hand on her arm in a protective manner.

'I see. Miss Petterson?'

'I can confirm what James — Mr Russell — has said,' said the governess in a quiet tone of voice, her face flushed, her hands trembling.

'We cannot afford to be seen in public, it would be the ruin of both of us. That was why I was not inclined to let you enter. I have Miss Petterson's interests at heart. You must understand that, Ravenscroft,' continued Russell.

'So that was why you went up to the church that afternoon?' asked Ravenscroft.

'Yes, I knew that Jane would be there. We had arranged to meet at three o'clock. I waited inside the church. Miss Petterson arrived a few minutes later.'

'I see, Mr Russell. This certainly puts a new complexion on the case. How long were you and Miss Petterson inside the church together?' asked Ravenscroft.

'It must have been for ten or fifteen minutes,' offered the governess.

'And all this time your charge was outside?'

'Yes. It was important that Mildred did not see us together. We could not risk that she would tell her father.'

'Plenty of time for her to have been taken,' muttered Crabb.

'I know, our behaviour was negligent. I thought Mildred was happy and safe outside. I was mistaken. I cannot forgive myself for what I did,' replied the governess beginning to cry.

'There, my dear. You were not to know that all that would happen. If anyone is to blame for all this, then it is I, Inspector, for placing Miss Petterson in a compromising situation' said Russell putting a comforting arm round her shoulder.

'Mr Russell, do you still maintain that you saw Old John in the churchyard when you entered the church?' asked Ravenscroft.

'Why, yes.'

'And you, Miss Petterson — did you see Old John when you entered the church?'

'No. Had John been there, I would not have let Mildred play there alone. John is harmless, I know, but—'

'He could have been hiding behind one of the stones, or round the other side of the building?' interrupted Crabb.

'Yes, I suppose so. You don't think John has taken Mildred?' asked the governess.

'I don't know what to think,' said Ravenscroft. 'What happened when you came out of the church?'

'I called for Mildred, and when I realized that she was not there, I ran back into the church and told Mr Russell.'

'And what did you do next, Mr Russell?' asked Ravenscroft.

'I ran out into the churchyard and together we made a quick search of the grounds. When we realized that Mildred was no longer there, it was decided that I would go down towards the town to see if she had wandered off there, whilst Jane, Miss Petterson I mean, returned to the house in case Mildred had gone there.'

'Tell me, Mr Russell, when you searched the churchyard was Old John still there?' asked Ravenscroft.

'No, the churchyard was empty,' replied Russell.

'Were you and Miss Petterson in the habit of meeting together inside the church? It is very important that we know.'

Russell looked at the governess before replying. 'Yes, we have met there on the same day of the week, and at the same time, for the past three weeks.'

'And was Miss Chilton with you on each of these occasions?'

'Yes,' replied the governess.

'And was she left outside on each occasion?'

'Yes.'

'Then it is possible that her abductor may have met and conversed with the young lady before on one of these days?'

'Yes, I suppose that might . . . oh no, you think that she knew the person who took her away?' asked Miss Petterson.

'Thank you, Mr Russell. You would not object if we made a thorough search of your buildings?' Asked Ravenscroft ignoring the last reply.

'Yes, I do mind actually. I mind very much indeed. We have told you the truth,' snapped Russell.

'James, it can do no harm,' said the governess attempting to placate the farmer.

Russell nodded, and Ravenscroft and Crabb began to leave the room.

'It would have been more helpful if you had told us the truth from the start of our inquiries, Miss Petterson. A great deal of valuable time has been lost,' said Ravenscroft crossly.

'I am sorry,' said the governess looking down at the floor.

'Miss Petterson did not want anyone to learn of our association. Chilton is a spiteful, revengeful man. He would have taken great pleasure in ruining us both,' added Russell.

'That's as may be. One more question, Mr Russell. How long have you and Miss Petterson been meeting like this?' asked Ravenscroft.

'We have been meeting for the past three months. Why do you ask?' replied Russell.

'No particular reason. Thank you.'

* * *

An hour later Ravenscroft and Crabb made their way back towards Vines Lane.

'Nothing sir. No sign of the girl in any of the outbuildings,' said Crabb.

'It would appear so, Tom,' sighed Ravenscroft.

'Of course they could be holding her elsewhere.'

'They could, but I still do not see why they would have taken the girl. At least we now know why Miss Petterson made up that story concerning the hymn books. The only reason she went into the church was to meet her lover. The fact that she then remained in the church for longer than she said, gave ample time for whoever took the girl to effect an escape. If only she had admitted the truth earlier, it would have saved us all a great deal of time,' said an annoyed Ravenscroft.

'We could arrest her for wasting police time,' suggested Crabb.

'Our Miss Petterson seems to be making quite a habit of not telling us the truth. First, all that nonsense about going into the church to see what hymns had been chosen, then her deception in using her sister's references to secure employment, and now we find that she has been carrying on an association with Mr Russell. We have more than enough to take her in for closer questioning, but I don't believe that would get us anywhere. All we can hope is that she has now finally told us the truth. There is one thing that still puzzles me though.'

'What is that sir?'

'If Russell and the governess are romantically attached, why does she not leave Sir Charles's employment and marry Russell? I know that Russell and Chilton are enemies, but surely that would be of no matter.'

'Perhaps Russell has no money to marry the woman, or he has not summoned up enough courage to propose to her yet?'

'You could be right.'

'There is always the possibility that Mildred caught Russell and the governess in the church, and that she then had to be silenced?' suggested Crabb.

'You mean they killed her because they feared she would tell her father all about their secret meetings?'

'After they killed the girl, Russell could have taken the body somewhere, whilst the governess raised the alarm at the house?'

'That is possible I suppose, but there would seem to be two things against your idea, Tom. Firstly I cannot see them killing the girl just to keep their assignation secret, and secondly if Russell had killed the girl how would he have transported the body from the churchyard and along Vines Lane in broad daylight?'

'He could have hidden the body in undergrowth and come back for it after dark and buried it somewhere.'

'No Tom, I just cannot accept that. I believe we can discount the theory, for the time being, that Russell and the governess are behind this abduction of Mildred Chilton. Whoever was responsible for her abduction, merely took advantage of the fact that the couple were inside the church for several minutes. One thing we have learnt however, is that Old John was in the churchyard when Russell arrived there and, although he was not there when Russell and Miss Petterson later searched for Miss Chilton, he may have witnessed the abduction of the girl.'

'He could have taken the girl himself?' suggested Crabb.

'I cannot see why.'

'He could have been sacked all those years ago from Hill Court, and is getting his own back?'

'If that were the case, why wait all these years? If he was harbouring some grudge against his former employer he would surely have acted sooner. No, I don't think Old John took the girl, but he may know who did. We must find him as soon as possible.'

'Where do we look sir?'

'The churchyard — that is where he spends most of his time. If Old John did see the girl being taken, he could prove a valuable witness.'

CHAPTER NINE

LEDBURY AND DROITWICH

'Crabb and I have searched every inch of that church and churchyard for that wretched man and nowhere could we find him,' said a frustrated Ravenscroft throwing his spoon down into the empty soup bowl.

'Samuel, I have never seen you so annoyed,' replied Lucy seeking to placate her husband.

Ravenscroft had returned home to Ledbury later that evening, and he and Lucy had just finished the first course of their dinner.

'Where is the wretched man? Yesterday he was everywhere; now he has just vanished. I have left two of the men in the churchyard in case he shows up there overnight. They won't thank me for being deprived of their families on a night like this.'

'I am sure he will turn up tomorrow,' said Lucy trying to sound reassuring.

'Confound the fellow!'

'Shall I ring for the mutton?'

'Yes. I'm sorry. I have been entirely selfish, being involved so dreadfully with this wretched case, that I have neglected the anxiety that you must have been feeling, after your visit to Droitwich. It must have been awful for you to have discovered the suicide of that other woman.'

Lucy said nothing, but looked down at her plate.

'My dear, I know that you, above all others, sympathize with these women, that you feel for their predicament, that you want to do all that you can for them—'

'Oh, Samuel, I did so much want to find those poor children, and reunite them with their mothers, but one mother is already dead — committed suicide, the newspaper report said,' cried Lucy. 'Now it has all come to nothing!'

'There, my dear. Please do not cry,' said Ravenscroft rising from the table and drawing his wife closer to him, resting her tear-stained face on his chest. 'I promise you that once this case is over, I will do all that is within my power to resolve the question of these missing children. If your Mrs Huddlestone is nowhere to be found in Cheltenham, there must be other towns where she can be located. Perhaps Mr Shorter will be able to find his missing piece of paper, and all will be well. In the meantime, you must remain hopeful.'

'Yes, I suppose so, but what am I to tell Miss Corbett? That she may never see her child again? That she has been the victim of some cruel hoax?'

'I know. I know,' said Ravenscroft trying to sound reassuring. 'Let's wait another day before we contact Miss Corbett. As you said, this John fellow might well be found tomorrow and then we shall learn who has taken Miss Chilton. Perhaps there is some connection between all these missing children?'

'Oh, do you think so?' asked Lucy drying her eyes.

'I know the Huddlestones have taken babies who have been only a few weeks old, and the Chilton girl is nine years old; there does not seem to be an obvious connection, except for the fact that the maid who committed suicide after giving her baby to the Huddlestones worked at Hill Court. Nevertheless, it may be that the Huddlestones learnt about the Chilton family through their association with Belinda

Parkes and decided to kidnap their daughter. Everything is possible I suppose, and until we have caught Old John we won't know the truth of the matter.'

'I suppose you're right,' said Lucy recovering her composure.

'Let us see what tomorrow brings, my dear.'

'Yes. Of course. You are quite right. We are being unduly pessimistic. You must be hungry and the mutton will be getting cold,' said Lucy picking up the bell and ringing it.

Ravenscroft returned to his seat, knowing that he had done everything he could to address his wife's fears, but also keenly aware that unless he found the old man by the next morning he would be no nearer to solving the mystery of the missing children. He realized that time was now against him, that there were no further lines of inquiry available, and that each day's delay only increased the probability that the children would not be found alive.

* * *

As soon as Ravenscroft alighted from the trap, he knew that the case had taken a turn for the worse. A group of uniformed officers were huddled together at the side of the canal near the lock gate. He prayed that it was not the Chilton girl they had found. No, not the girl. It must not be the girl.

'Inspector,' said one of the men stepping back from the huddle of men. 'We fished him out of the water this morning.'

Ravenscroft knelt down and pulled off the body's covering.

'Old John!' exclaimed Crabb.

'Been in the water all night, I would say,' said one of the group.

'Sorry, you are?' asked Ravenscroft of the soberly dressed man standing nearby.

'Doctor Staples. I have a practice here in Droitwich. One of your men summoned me this morning; we did not want to move the body until you had arrived.'

'Doctor Staples, I am pleased to make your acquaintance,' said Ravenscroft standing up and shaking the practioner's hand. 'I am glad you are here, and grateful you left the body where it was until my arrival. You say he must have been in the water all night?'

'That is my opinion,' replied the grey haired physician.

'Death by drowning then,' observed Crabb.

'I don't think so, Constable. There is evidence of a rather nasty blow on the back of the head. Here,' said Staples indicating a large area of discoloured red stain on the deceased man's head.

'He could have hit his head on the side of the lock gate when he fell into the water?' suggested Ravenscroft, but knew that this was improbable.

'There is always that possibility, of course, but in my opinion someone dealt him a heavy blow before pushing him into the water.'

'I am inclined to agree with you, Doctor Staples,' said Ravenscroft staring down at the dead man's injuries.

'Poor old fellow,' said Crabb. 'He never did anyone any harm.'

'As you say, it must have been done when it was dark. If he had been killed during daylight someone who was walking along the towpath who would have seen the crime.'

'Will it now be in order to take the body to the mortuary?' asked Staples.

'Yes of course,' replied Ravenscroft giving instructions to the men. 'Doctor, I wonder if you would allow me a few more minutes of your time?'

'Certainly. How can I help?'

'I assume you have been a doctor here for a great number of years?'

'Dear me, do I appear to be that old?' smiled Staples.

'No. I'm sorry. I did not mean any offence.'

'There was none taken. Yes, I have practiced in the town for the past forty years. I wish I could say that it felt only like yesterday that I first came to Droitwich, but no, it certainly feels like two score years.'

'Then you know most of the people in this neighbourhood?' asked Ravenscroft.

'Yes, I suppose so.'

'What can you tell me about Old John?'

'Harmless enough fellow. Completely unhinged, of course.'

'Had he always been in that condition?' asked Ravenscroft as the two men walked away from the towpath.

'No. He worked as a groom at Hill Court for many years, but then he lost his employment there, about ten years ago if I remember correctly. After that he just seemed to shut himself off from everybody and everything. He became something of a recluse and quite lost his mind, the poor fellow.'

'Do you know why he was dismissed?'

'Sorry, Inspector, I cannot help you there.'

'Was Miss Belinda Parkes one of your patients?'

'Ah, the maid at Hill Court. Why do you ask?'

'The disappearance of her infant child may have some bearing on this case.'

'I cannot see why,' said Staples, a perplexed look on his face.

'I would be obliged if you could tell me all you know about Miss Parkes,' smiled Ravenscroft, hoping that the doctor might provide some useful information.

'Miss Parkes was certainly a patient of mine. She had felt compelled to give her baby away, and became very distressed when she was unable to recover the child.'

'Did she tell you anything about the people to whom she gave the baby?'

'No. She never mentioned them by name. A very sad case. The next we heard was that she had thrown herself into the canal.'

'Did you examine the body when it was recovered?'

'Yes certainly, Inspector, but no, there was no foul play, if that is what you are suggesting. The girl had clearly committed suicide due to a deranged mind.'

'What can you tell me of Sir Charles Chilton?' asked Ravenscroft.

'Well, you have met Sir Charles, so you know what he is like. Let us say that he is a man who does not tolerate fools gladly.'

'A self-made man?'

'Partly so. He inherited the family business from his father, Sir Christopher. It was he who really established the business. There is a tragedy there, of course.'

'Oh, what is that?' asked Ravenscroft his curiosity aroused.

'Well, there was an elder brother, Peter Chilton. A perfect gentleman on all counts, very easy going, liked by everyone, but he died tragically young, and so the business eventually passed to his younger brother, Sir Charles.'

'The servants said that Peter had died quite suddenly?'

'Yes. I did not attend him of course. I believe he died on a business trip whilst in London. The body was bought back to Droitwich, and rests in the family vault in Dodderhill churchyard.'

'I understand, Doctor, that Lady Chilton was once engaged to Peter?'

'That was indeed so, but as you know she married Sir Charles.'

'Do you attend Lady Chilton?' asked Ravenscroft.

'She is one of my patients indeed, but you must appreciate I cannot discuss her illness with you,' replied Staples defensively.

'I understand, doctor. How long has her illness persisted?' queried Ravenscroft.

'I am sorry, I cannot discuss this any further. You must excuse me. I have patients to attend to,' replied the doctor abruptly, before striding away in the direction of the town.

'I think I may have upset the good doctor,' said Ravenscroft as Crabb joined him.

'Oh, why was that, sir?'

'I asked about Lady Chilton's illness, but no matter, have the men taken Old John to the mortuary?'

'Yes sir. Do you want to follow on, sir?'

'No. I don't think we can gain anything by further examining the corpse. I wonder why Old John was killed?'

'Perhaps the killer thought that the old tramp had seen him abduct the girl, and if we found him first he would tell us all he knew?' suggested Crabb.

'I think you are probably right, Tom. Killed before he could tell us the truth. One thing is now certain.'

'What's that sir?'

'We now know that whoever killed Old John must still be in the area — and if the killer is still in the vicinity, and not on some barge half-way to Birmingham, then Mildred Chilton must also be quite close. Tom, I want you to see that every available man is despatched to search all the empty buildings around the town. The girl must be somewhere, and I am determined to find her. I fear that if we do not find Miss Chilton soon it may be too late. The person who took her has already killed once; he may well do so again.'

'What will you do sir?'

'I will go back to the house. I am interested to know why Old John left his work at Hill Court.'

* * *

As Ravenscroft made his way through the gate that led into the kitchen garden, he observed the cook standing by one of the vegetable patches.

'Good morning to you, Mrs Greenway. Are you choosing some vegetables for the table?'

'Good morning, Inspector. I am indeed. These carrots should be ready for digging quite soon. We have just heard the news about poor John.'

'News travels fast. I was hoping to have a few moments of your time, if I may,' said Ravenscroft.

'Certainly sir. How can I be of assistance to you?'

'I understand that Old John used to work here?'

'Yes, he was employed as a groom, for many years. I cannot tell you much about him though. He always kept himself aloof from the rest of us servants, preferring to spend most of his free time in the stables. He even had a room there. I think the only person he struck up any kind of relationship was with young Master Peter. They spent a lot of time with each other. They often went riding together.'

'What kind of boy was Master Peter?'

'Lovely boy he was. Liked by everyone he was. I did not have that much to do with him of course, being only the cook. He was bought up by Nanny Jones, but she retired many years ago to her cottage in Elmbridge.'

'Can you tell me why Old John was dismissed from his employment?' asked Ravenscroft anxious to know more.

'It was shortly after the death of Master Peter. We could not understand why he was asked to leave so suddenly. I suppose Sir Charles took a dislike to him,' replied Mrs Greenway.

'I would be obliged if you could try to remember. It may be important for our investigations.'

The cook looked down at the ground, deep in thought for some moments, before speaking. 'I remember that Master Peter went up to London on business, and that shortly afterwards Sir Charles received news that his older brother had died quite suddenly. Old John and Sir Charles immediately went up to London, and returned three days later with the coffin. It were a very sad time, sir. All the house was in mourning. The old master, Sir Christopher, was very infirm by that time, and took to his bed. He never got over the death of his beloved son. Master Peter was buried in the churchyard, and a few days later we were told that Old John had been cast out. That is all I can remember of what happened.'

'Old John never said why he had been forced to leave?' asked Ravenscroft.

'No. I know that Sir Charles said that if ever John came back onto his property, we were to inform the local police, and have him arrested.'

'That would appear to be quite harsh treatment?'

'We thought so at the time, but of course we dared not speak up for John, in case the master took exception, and we lost our positions as well.'

'Quite, I understand.'

'That is all I can tell you, Inspector. I am sorry that I could not have been more helpful,' said the cook.

'On the contrary you have been most informative, Mrs Greenway. Most informative indeed. I thank you for your time,' said Ravenscroft raising his hat as he began to walk back through the garden door.

CHAPTER TEN

LEDBURY AND WORCESTER

Lucy closed the lid of the piano, unable to concentrate on the music before her, her thoughts constantly returned to the whereabouts of the missing children; she was saddened by her powerlessness to do anything to resolve the situation.

The door opened and the maid entered the room.

'Please ma'am, there's a rather strange looking man who insists on seeing you.'

'Did he give you his name?'

'Says his name is Shorter.'

'Clement Shorter at your service again, my dear Mrs Ravenscroft,' said the newspaperman brushing past the maid and striding up to Lucy and shaking her hand vigorously. 'So pleased to make your acquaintance again, my good lady.'

'My dear Mr Shorter, how pleasant to see you again,' replied Lucy somewhat taken aback by the new arrival's dramatic entrance. 'Do take a seat. Perhaps you would care to take some refreshment?'

'No time for refreshments, or even a seat ma'am. I have it here!' exclaimed Shorter brandishing a piece of paper, which he had just removed from his coat pocket.

'You have found the address?'

'Indeed, my dear Mrs Ravenscroft. That which was lost has been found. The errant lamb has returned to the fold!'

'Oh well done,' said an enthusiastic Lucy.

'After your visit, I felt compelled to launch an expedition to find the rogue paper, and after an hour or two of searching through the jungle of accumulated articles and discarded ephemera, there it was, inside my copy of The Post Office Directory. Page 372 to be precise. Why it should have secreted itself there must alas remain a mystery,' said the excitable newspaperman, the words tumbling out one after another in quick succession.

'And what address does our record show?' asked Lucy anxiously interrupting the flow of words.

'It appears that our Mrs Huddlestone resides not all that distance from where we are at present. Worcester to be precise. 16A Inkerman Street. Shades of the Crimea, I detect. There is not a moment to lose, my dear lady. I believe the next train for that place leaves in just twenty minutes.'

'Then we shall certainly go and seek out this Mrs Huddlestone, but perhaps I am detaining you from your work?'

'This is my work, my dear lady! I have a duty to my readers to seek out the truth, to right the great wrongs of our society, to overturn all stones, to break through the braken and jungle, to explore those unknown darkened areas of the world! And if I can be of assistance to you in this great matter, albeit in a sideways capacity, then I will pleased to do so. I see that all this has the making of a good story.'

'Then I would be delighted if you would accompany me, Mr Shorter. Shall we go?'

* * *

Later that morning, Lucy and Shorter made their way down the narrow streets of the district in the town of Worcester known to its inhabitants as the Arboretum. To Lucy it seemed as though the smoke from the various chimneys and the nearby factories, which hung over the rows of insignificant terraced dwellings, served only to heighten the oppressive gloom and eerie silence of the area.

'Ah, here we are. This appears to be Inkerman Street,' announced Shorter pausing at the corner of one of the narrow roads. 'Now, my good lady, are you sure that you wish to undertake this visit alone? Who knows what lies hidden behind such closed doors; what secrets are waiting to be revealed from the other side of half-drawn ancient curtains?'

'I must confess that I am somewhat apprehensive, Mr Shorter, but if we are to avoid suspicion, it is better that I go by myself. If this Mrs Huddlestone does reside at this address, then it is to be hoped that the two infant children may still be in her care,' replied Lucy.

'Then I wish you well, Mrs Ravenscroft. In order that I am not seen by the inhabitants of the house, I will take the liberty of waiting round the corner. Be sure to call upon me, my dear good lady, if the situation so demands it.'

'Thank you Mr Shorter, you are most kind. I am sure I will not be long.'

As Lucy walked down the narrow road, she noticed that her hands had begun to shake with trepidation at what she might find behind the closed door of number 16A Inkerman Street. Would she be able to find the missing infants of Alice Corbett and the deceased chambermaid from Droitwich, within the confines of the house — and if the children were there, how would she be able to secure their release? Would she also be able to discover the whereabouts of Mildred Chilton and to reunite her with her parents? What kind of woman would the unknown Amelia Huddlestone turn out to be — and would she accept the story she had formulated in her mind, or reject it out of hand?

She hesitated before bringing her gloved hand down on the wooden door. Receiving no reply, she considered the possibility that her visit might prove in vain — perhaps the Huddlestones had departed some time ago, leaving the house empty? But then she thought she detected a brief movement of a curtain in the upstairs window, and felt reassured to repeat her action once more.

Presently she heard the sound of footsteps in the distance, and after what seemed to Lucy to be an eternity, the door slowly opened a few inches.

'Good morning. I am looking for Mrs Huddlestone,' said Lucy rather hesitantly after clearing her throat.

'Who wants her?' asked the speaker opening the door another inch or two.

'My name is Ravenscroft. I have come about the advertisement.'

'What advertisement?' asked the grey-haired woman adopting a defensive manner.

'In the Droitwich Guardian. The advertisement stated that you were looking for a child to bring up as your own.'

'How did you know of my address?' asked the woman eying Lucy.

'I know that I should have replied to your advertisement at the time, but the editor said that all the responses had been sent on to this address, and as my plight is somewhat urgent, I thought you would not mind if I applied to you in person,' said Lucy, conscious that she was stumbling over her words as the hard faced woman stared intently into her eyes.

'You best come in then,' said the woman, softening her tone, and indicating that Lucy should enter the building. 'You will have to excuse us, we were not expecting visitors.'

'I am sorry for the intrusion, but you are the only person I can turn to,' said Lucy following the woman into the front room of the house.

'In trouble are we?'

Lucy taken aback by the sudden abrasive tone of the question, uttered, 'I don't know what to do.'

'Sit down there, my dear,' said her hostess indicating one of the chairs grouped round the table. 'Granny, will you take that child away.'

Lucy noticed an old woman, sitting at one of the chairs, and a thin delicate looking boy cowering in the corner of the room.

'Is this your boy?' asked Lucy.

The child, whom Lucy judged to be no more than seven years of age, gave the older woman a frightened look as she stood up and grasped his arm rudely, before the two of them left the room together.

'Give him some food, Granny,' shouted the woman. 'The lad's not mine. He is staying with us for a few days whilst his mother is away.'

'I see. Do you have any children of your own?' asked Lucy.

'Full of questions ain't we? I thought you had read the advertisement?' replied the woman curtly.

'Yes of course, how remiss of me. I am sorry for your loss.'

'The good Lord took her away. Not for us to question the decisions of the Almighty. There was little we could do,' said the woman without emotion. 'Now what can I do for you, my dear?'

'I don't quite know how to begin,' said Lucy removing a handkerchief from her pocket and bringing it up to her nose.

'Take your time my dear,' said her hostess adopting a more sympathetic tone.

'I am engaged as a governess to a gentleman of some importance in the county.'

'Thought as much. You looked too grand to be a chambermaid. Bit too free with his ways was he?'

'It was the gentleman's nephew,' replied Lucy dabbing the corner of one eye.

'Usually the way. Men can be so thoughtless. You are not the first to fall for such a man, nor will you be the last. Go on.'

'He promised me so much. I was foolish to believe that he would ever care for me. The child was born a month ago. The master said he was prepared to overlook my indiscretion, but on no account would he take on the child. I didn't know what to do. If I am dismissed from my position, we will both be penniless and I will never be able to find future employment. I don't want to give up my baby, but I can see no other way. Then one of the maids in the house remembered your advertisement in the newspaper. Am I to late? Have you found a child already?'

'There, there, now my dear, don't distress yourself so. The good Lord has sent you to me in your hour of need,' replied the woman placing a comforting hand on Lucy's arm. 'We will see what can be done.'

'Oh, thank goodness.'

'You have a little boy or girl?'

'A girl.'

'Does she have a name?'

'Maria.'

'A pleasant enough name. My child was Clarissa Ann. Such a pretty name, but the good Lord took her away to a far more holy place. I know she is well provided for in the afterlife, but the sadness leaves a lonely chill behind.'

'I am sorry.'

'But now you have come to bring light into our family. Mr Huddlestone will be so delighted when I tell him our good news. He works as a railway goods agent on the Midland Railway you know. Such a demanding occupation. You would not object to our calling your child, Clarissa Ann. It would so remind Mr Huddlestone of our own dear daughter.'

'No, I suppose not,' replied Lucy looking down sadly at her hands and the twisted handkerchief in her lap.

'Of course, we would want some form of remuneration for our taking on the child. Mr Huddlestone would insist on that. Just to help with our expenses.'

'Yes, I understand.'

'Fifteen guineas.'

'Fifteen guineas!' exclaimed Lucy.

'If you think that is too much, then perhaps you had better leave,' said the woman, abruptly rising and moving her chair back from the table.

'No, no,' said Lucy quickly. 'I did not mean to cause offence. Please help me. I have no one else to turn to. I have the money.'

'Good, and if you have any items of clothing belonging to the child—'

'Yes.'

'There would have to be one more condition. Once you have handed over your baby, it would be better if you were not to see her for at least six months or more. We find it is better for the child. It would be very upsetting for her if you kept visiting, I am sure you understand that, my dear,' smiled Mrs Huddlestone.

'Yes, I suppose so.'

'Good, then that is all settled. When would you like to bring the child?' asked Mrs Huddlestone in a business-like manner, indicating that the meeting was drawing to its conclusion.

'Would tomorrow morning be acceptable? My employer is anxious to avoid any scandal,' replied Lucy standing up.

'I understand.'

Lucy looked across to the corner of the room, where a red shawl lay crumpled on the floor. Had not Alice Corbett mentioned that she had given away her daughter in a red shawl?

The woman caught her stare. 'Something wrong, my dear?'

'The shawl, red,' she muttered. 'It is just that red is not my favourite colour. It has so many bad memories for me.'

'You should not let such things disturb you, my dear,' said Amelia Huddlestone giving her a stern look.

'What was that noise?' cried out Lucy.

'What noise my dear?'

'I thought I heard a child crying. Somewhere upstairs,' said Lucy anxiously.

'I think you are mistaken, my dear. I have no other children here besides the boy you saw when you came in,' replied Mrs Huddlestone quickly showing Lucy out of the room.

'I'm sure I heard a child,' persisted Lucy.

'Next door. They are a noisy family. Nothing for you to worry about. Shall we say ten tomorrow morning?'

'Yes. Ten. That would be most acceptable.'

'Then good day to you. What did you say your name was?'

'Ravenscroft, Mrs — sorry, Miss Ravenscroft.'

The woman gave Lucy a curious glance before opening the door and ushering her out into the street.

* * *

'Well my dear Mrs Ravenscroft, what did you discover?' asked Shorter eagerly as he and Lucy made their way back towards the railway station in Foregate Street.

'I told her our story, that I had been foolish in my attentions, and that I now wanted to be free of my child.'

'Excellent!' said an excited Shorter.

'I think she believed me, although I cannot be absolutely sure. I thought she was very much on her guard. Such a hard, grained face and cold eyes; it was difficult to understand what she might possibly have been thinking. She wanted fifteen guineas to take the child.'

'A princely sum indeed.'

'I said I would return at ten tomorrow morning, with the child.'

'Quick thinking indeed — but you don't have a child of that age, I presume?'

'I have a son who is a few months old. I told her I had a girl. I will speak with my husband tonight. He will know how best to proceed. I am sure he will want to keep the appointment for me.'

'Capital, my dear lady. Capital.'

'There was another boy in the house, a frightened, pitiful child, with large wistful eyes, about seven years of age, and an older woman who seemed to be looking after him. Oh, how I felt for that child; I wanted to reach out there and then, and take him away with me. Then when I was leaving, I was sure I heard a small child crying upstairs. Oh, Mr Shorter I am sure she has the babies hidden upstairs! Perhaps that is where young Mildred Chilton is too, imprisoned against her will. I must return to Ledbury, without delay and inform my husband as soon as he comes home. We must save the children,' said an agitated Lucy.

'Indeed we must my dear lady, but although I feel bound to help you at this very moment, I do not have the proper authority to enter the woman's house, despite any misgivings we might have,' said a sympathetic Shorter.

'I understand that we are powerless to act at present.'

'I am afraid I must wish you good day for the present, Mrs Ravenscroft. Deadlines to be met. Paper to be published. Clarence will be waiting for his supper. Always fish on a Friday. He gets particularly annoyed if he is kept waiting. Are you well, Mrs Ravenscroft? You look particularly drawn if you do not mind my saying.'

'Oh Mr Shorter, there was something else in that house that I found particularly unsettling.'

'What was that, my dear lady?'

'A terrible smell — a damp, decaying kind of smell, that seemed to linger in the room . . .'

* * *

Shortly before ten the following morning, Ravenscroft and Crabb made their way along Inkerman Street. The smoke from the nearby factories seemed to hang like a black cloud over the city, keeping the sun well hidden, and adding to the veil of damp gloom that drifted slowly across the Arboretum. A shabbily dressed man passed them on the other side of the street, seeking to restrain his large dog which growled in the detectives' direction.

'Let us see if we are able to keep Lucy's appointment. We will need to search the house thoroughly. If she has the children we will take her into custody. It may be difficult to prove a case against her — after all, the mothers parted with money for this Mrs Huddlestone to look after their unwanted children, but there is clear deception involved in this case, I am sure. The poor parlour maid in Droitwich is deceased, but we can hope to reunite Miss Corbett with her child. And who knows, we may find Mildred Chilton inside as well. Ah, here we are, Tom. Knock on the door, will you,' instructed Ravenscroft standing back and looking up at the upstairs window.

'No answer sir,' said Crabb after a few moments had elapsed.

'Knock again. If we don't get an answer this time, we will have to force open the door.'

'That won't do you any good. They've all left!'

Startled by the voice, Ravenscroft turned round to see an elderly woman, wearing an apron and shawl over a brown dress, standing in the street. 'I am sorry madam, but I don't quite understand.'

'Left they did. Late last night. All of them, gone,' sniffed the voice.

'And you are?' asked Ravenscroft.

'Who wants to know?'

'Police,' replied Crabb drawing himself up to his full height.

'Mrs Bannister. I lives next door but one, at number 14.'

'Mrs Bannister, you say that they all left last night. What time was that, to be precise?' asked Ravenscroft.

'About six. An hour or so after that posh looking lady turned up,' said the woman sniffing again.

'That must have been Lucy,' said Ravenscroft addressing Crabb. 'Tell me who exactly lived in the house, and how long had they been here?'

'Been here for about a year. There was the woman—'

'Mrs Huddlestone?' interjected Crabb.

'Don't know no Huddlestones. Said her name was Drew. Amelia Drew, that was her name. Then there was Granny,'

'That must be the old woman Lucy saw,' said Ravenscroft. 'Please go on.'

'Granny Thomson, that were her name. Never said anything, just stayed indoors all day looking after the boy she did.'

'A boy. How old was this boy?'

'About seven or eight. Frightened little child he was. I could not help feel sorry for him. They used to treat him terrible they did. Never seemed to give him enough food, or let him out to play with the other children,' replied the woman sniffing and beginning to move away.

'Was there anyone else?' asked Ravenscroft eagerly.

'There was a daughter. Used to come and visit sometimes, but not very often. Don't know much about her. Think her name was Polly. That's all.'

'Tell me, was there a small child — a baby perhaps?'

'Yes, a baby. They took the baby with them, when they left. I saw it was wrapped up in a shawl. Crying it was.'

'Can you tell me the colour of this shawl?' asked Ravenscroft eager to know more.

'I don't know do I? What do you want to know for anyway, they ain't done nothing has they?' sniffed the woman again.

'It is very important, Mrs Bannister,' emphasized Ravenscroft.

'Red. It were red.'

'Thank you. They didn't happen to say where they were going to, when they left yesterday evening, I suppose?' asked Ravenscroft.

'Not a word. They just upped and left, all of them.'

'Tell me, was there only just the one baby?'

'You wants to know a lot don't you?' said the woman blowing her nose noisily.

'It is very important that we know everything,' pressed Ravenscroft.

'There was another baby, just before this one arrived, but it died. She said it caught a chill, then had a fever. Poor mite. Don't know where they buried it.'

'Thank you, Mrs Bannister, you have been most helpful,' said Ravenscroft turning away.

'You don't want to know about the young girl then?' coughed the woman.

'What young girl?' asked Ravenscroft with great interest.

'Don't know her name. Arrived suddenly one day, shortly after they moved in. Never saw much of her. They kept her inside all day. Then Mrs Drew said she was gone away, unexpected like, and we never saw anything else of her.'

'How old was this girl,' asked Ravenscroft giving Crabb a concerned look.

'About six or seven I would say.'

'When was the last time you saw this girl?'

'As I said, I never saw much of her after she had arrived. Amelia, Mrs Drew, said she had gone, sudden like. This was about six months ago I suppose.'

'You have not seen another girl here, of about eight years of age? She may have arrived in the past few days?' asked an anxious Ravenscroft.

'No. There was only the one girl, the one that left.'

'Thank you once again for your information,' said Ravenscroft, as the woman made her way into her own house.

'Sounds serious, sir,' said Crabb.

'Confound it, Tom! Why didn't we come last night, as soon as Lucy told us her news? We might have been able to catch them all before they left,' said an annoyed Ravenscroft.

'Begging your pardon, sir, but we did not return to Ledbury until after eight o'clock. If Mrs Huddlestone and her party left just after six, we would have missed them anyway,' said Crabb trying to placate his superior officer.

'Yes, but the trail would have been warmer. They could be anywhere now.'

'Suppose you're right sir.'

'The child she speaks off cannot be Mildred Chilton, as that happened some months ago, but I don't like the sound of this at all, Tom. Put your shoulder to the door and see if it will yield.'

Crabb pushed hard against the woodwork, and after his second attempt the door gave way.

'This must the room where Lucy was interviewed by this Huddlestone/Drew woman, or whatever she calls herself,' said Ravenscroft looking round the sparsely furnished room. 'Take a look upstairs Tom, whilst I see if there is anything down here which might offer us a clue as to where they have gone to.'

'Right sir,' said Crabb quickly striding up the steps that led from the hall.

Ravenscroft looked around the room at the furniture, but could find nothing of a personal nature. A door at the back of the room opened up onto a smaller room and then a kitchen, where only a few unwashed pieces of crockery were to be found. A back door with a cracked pane of glass in its frame, opened out onto a small backyard, where a half empty bag of coal leaned against the outer wall.

'Nothing upstairs sir,' said Crabb returning to the room. 'They seem to have taken all their clothes and personal effects with them.'

'There is nothing down here either. Something Lucy said must have frightened them, hence their sudden departure. Clearly that woman has a lot to hide.'

'Terrible smell down here though, sir. Not so bad upstairs,' said Crabb twitching his nose.

'Yes, I must say that I noticed that as soon as we entered. I smelt that kind of smell once before some years ago in Whitechapel — oh, my God!' replied Ravenscroft suddenly bringing his handkerchief to his nose.

'Whatever is the matter sir?'

'See if we can locate the source of that terrible smell.'

'There is a cupboard under the stairs,' indicated Crabb.

Ravenscroft walked over to the cupboard and flung open the doors.

'Good God!' exclaimed Crabb as the two men recoiled. 'The smell is terrible.'

'See Tom, there is some earth here, as though someone has recently dug up the floor tiles. The floor has been disturbed. I think whatever is producing that awful smell must be under this earth. I think I spotted a shovel in the kitchen, will you get it Tom,' said Ravenscroft bringing his handkerchief again up to his nose.

'Shall I dig, sir?' asked Crabb returning from the kitchen holding the spade.

'If you can bear it, Tom,' said Ravenscroft stepping back from the cupboard area.

Crabb moved two or three shovels of earth away, before Ravenscroft cried out, 'Stop, Tom. I think we may have found something.'

Kneeling, Ravenscroft brushed the loose earth to one side with his gloved hand.

'Good grief sir, what is it!' cried out an ashen faced Crabb, dropping the spade on the floor with a clatter, his hands shaking.

'Bones, Tom — bones, and rotting flesh! If I am not mistaken I think we might have found the remains of that poor missing girl!'

CHAPTER ELEVEN

DROITWICH

As Crabb drove the trap round the winding lanes that lead from Worcester towards Droitwich, Ravenscroft remained deep in thought, oblivious to his ever changing surroundings. Three hours had passed since the discovery of the child's bones in the house in Inkerman Street — three hours of intense activity during which the remains had been taken away to the local mortuary, and the two men had sent out descriptions of the house's occupants to surrounding police stations. Crabb had made exhaustive enquiries at the Worcester railway stations in the hope that someone had witnessed the departure of the family, whilst Ravenscroft had interviewed the local cabmen — but on both accounts they met with no success. It was as if Amelia Drew, the old woman, and their charges, had vanished into thin air.

The doctor had been unable to say how the young girl had died, only that the corpse was several weeks old. Had she been deliberately killed by Amelia Drew, or allowed to starve to death, or had she died simply of natural causes? There was no way of telling, but if the child had been ill, and had died in a natural way, surely she would have been given a proper burial, rather than the makeshift resting place underneath the stairs of the miserable house. No, it seemed to Ravenscroft more than likely that she had been killed by the evil woman, and disposed of in a cruel despicable way, that was beyond any human understanding.

Then there was the question of the two infants — one of them had been taken away from the house, the other one had died shortly after its arrival there, but which one had lived, Alice Corbett's child or the baby of the deceased chambermaid from Droitwich? There was no way of telling which one had survived, and despite an extensive search of the house, no further remains had been uncovered. But what disturbed Ravenscroft the most was the thought of that poor half-starved boy whom Lucy had described to him in such vivid terms — could he be Amelia Drew's own son, or simply just another unwanted child that the woman had taken into her household? Either way, it seemed a cruel life to be enclosed within the walls of that house, to be seen by no one, and to live continually in fear of its adult occupants. And who was Granny Thompson — what part had she played in all this? Was she related to the Drew woman, or just someone employed to take charge of the children?

Ravenscroft feared for the safety of the two remaining children. If Amelia Drew — or Huddlestone as she had called herself in her dealings with Alice Corbett — had killed the girl whose remains they'd found under the stairs, and possibly the infant as well, she would have little hesitation in ending the lives of the boy and the infant child, to say nothing of poor Mildred Chilton. It was imperative that the family be found as soon as possible, but without any lines of enquiry to follow actively, there was little that he and Crabb could do at the present, other than leave the Worcester police in charge of further investigations and to wait for a possible sighting of the family there, or in the outlying areas.

'A penny for your thoughts, sir,' interjected Crabb.

'I can't stop thinking about that poor girl under the stairs. I wish we knew how she had died.'

'We have done all we can at present,' said Crabb making a half-hearted attempt to break the depression of his superior officer.

'It seems a terrible way to die, and to be buried under a pile of earth beneath the stairs of that unholy house, without ceremony or remembrance. What agonies that poor child might have suffered — it does not bear thinking about.'

'It is a pity we did not arrive sooner.'

'Yes, if only we had arrived last night we might have caught them in the act of leaving, or at least they would not have travelled far, but now another day has passed and they must have effected a thorough escape. All we can hope is that someone finds them sooner rather than later; we seem to have our hands more than full at the moment, Tom. I hope that the Worcester Constabulary can track down the woman and make an arrest. Unfortunately we still have Mildred Chilton to find.'

'Do you think this Drew woman has Miss Chilton in her clutches?' asked Crabb.

'It does not appear so from what that woman in the street said, but in the absence of any other lines of enquiry, I suppose we must consider the distinct possibility that she was taken by that awful woman.'

'What do we do next, sir?'

'Do you know, Tom, I have not the faintest idea as to how we are to proceed. All our enquiries seem to have come to an end, so until we can find out where that Drew woman and the others went when they left Worcester last night, we cannot do anything. I wonder whether Mildred Chilton was with them? Do you know I find it very strange that none of the lock keepers, nor any of the canal people, reported anything unusual on the canal. If whoever took Mildred left the town along the waterway, they would surely have been seen. Any stranger with a finely dressed nine-year-old girl, would have stood out like a sore thumb in such surroundings,' continued Ravenscroft.

'I thought you said that whoever took Miss Chilton must have remained in the town, as he, or she, must have been there to kill Old John?' suggested Crabb.

'Yes, I suppose you're right, Tom, and yet all our searches in empty building in the town have yielded nothing. I am just clutching at sinking straws, Tom.'

'Straws don't sink sir; they float.'

Ravenscroft said nothing as he turned away.

A few minutes later Crabb bought the horse to a stand-still outside the police station at Droitwich.

'We might as well see whether any telegrams have arrived for us,' said Ravenscroft without any degree of expectancy, as he stepped down from the trap and walked into the station.

'Any news,' asked Ravenscroft addressing the uniformed officer who was busily writing in a large ledger on his desk.

'No news of the missing girl, but this has just arrived for you sir,' said the officer handing his superior an envelope.

Ravenscroft tore open the envelope and read the enclosed telegram—

'POSSIBLE SIGHTING OF MISSING GIRL. LOCK KEEPER, TARDEBIGGE.'

'Where is Tardebigge?' asked Ravenscroft eagerly.

'It is on the Worcester–Birmingham canal sir, just north of where it joins up with the Droitwich Junction Canal from here,' replied the constable.

'How far is it?'

'About eight or nine miles as the crow flies sir.'

'Can you take us there?'

'Indeed I can, sir. May I ask—'

'Possible sighting of Mildred Chilton. Come with us, man. Crabb, harness the horse again,' interrupted Ravenscroft, quickly leading the way out of the station and jumping into the trap.

Their journey took them along the road that ran beside the canal, until they reached the hamlet of Hanbury. Here Crabb swung the trap left onto another road which headed northwards along country lanes; their route took them away from the canal for a while, but followed the railway line. Some buildings soon came into view.

'Stoke Prior sir,' said the constable indicating the name of the village where the road, railway line and canal all seemed to converge together.

'How much further to this Tardebigge?' asked an impatient Ravenscroft.

'The flight of locks starts about a mile or so ahead of us, sir.'

'Then let us hope that we are in time to rescue Mildred Chilton,' replied Ravenscroft. 'How far is it to Worcester, down the canal, from this point?'

'About ten miles I would say, sir,' replied the constable.

'Time enough for Drew and her party to have travelled up here along the canal since yesterday evening. We should have considered that they would leave Worcester this way. We were too busy, Tom, checking the trains and cabs,' remarked Ravenscroft reproaching himself for having not thought of this line of enquiry.

Crabb urged the horse onwards along the side of the canal, until a lock gate and keeper's cottage came into view.

'Stop here!' shouted Ravenscroft observing that the lock keeper was sitting on an old bench outside the building. 'Are you the gentleman who sent us the telegram?' he said addressing the keeper.

'If you are the police, then that be so,' replied the man drawing on an old wooden pipe at the corner of his mouth.

'I'm Inspector Ravenscroft investigating the abduction of Miss Mildred Chilton. Your telegram reports a possible sighting of the girl,' said Ravenscroft dismounting from the trap.

'That's what I said. Man, woman and girl on one of the boats.'

'Can you tell me whether the girl you saw was this one?' asked Ravenscroft removing the photograph of the missing girl from his coat pocket and passing it over to the keeper.

'Well?' asked an impatient Ravenscroft after a few moments had elapsed.

'I don't rightly know. I didn't get a good look at her. I didn't have me spectacles on at the time.'

'For goodness sake, man, is this the girl or not?'

'Well I thinks so, although I wouldn't like to swear it were her. Never seen them, nor their boat before on these waters. They was certainly acting strange,' replied the man taking another draw on his pipe before landing a large spit on the ground near Ravenscroft's feet.

'What do you mean, they were acting strange?' asked Ravenscroft feeling his patience being truly tried as he retrieved the photograph.

'Well, when they went through the lock gate, the girl was standing on the deck of the barge, and when I looked across at her, the man pushed her down through the hatch, quickly like, as though he didn't want me to see her close up, if you gets my meaning.'

'You say there was a man, woman and young girl on board. Did you happen to see or hear either a young boy or a baby?'

'No, there was no babby, nor any young lad.'

'They could have been below, sir,' suggested Crabb.

'How long ago was all this?' asked Ravenscroft.

'About four or five hours ago,' replied the man spitting again onto the ground, and narrowly missing Crabb's left boot.

'Four or five hours ago!' exclaimed Ravenscroft. 'They could be half way to Birmingham by now.'

'Ah well, that's where you be wrong. There be nearly another thirty lock gates to get through before they gets through Tardebigge. They won't have got far.'

'Thirty lock gates?' queried Crabb.

'It's the incline see. Has to be thirty lock gates. It's called the Tardebigge Flight; one of the seven wonders of the English canal system.'

'Then we may still be in time to save Mildred Chilton. Quickly man, describe this barge to us?' urged Ravenscroft.

'An old decrepit tub it was. Red with green line round it. Called the *Grasshopper* I believe.'

'Tie up the horse, Tom. We may do better on foot,' instructed Ravenscroft before setting off at a brisk pace along the towpath, closely followed by Crabb and the other constable.

'And a good day to you as well, sir,' grumbled the lock keeper, before aiming another spittle of saliva in the horses' direction.

As the trio ran along the towpath they looked across at the various barges making their way through the numerous lock gates.

'The lockkeeper said they couldn't have got far,' shouted Ravenscroft.

'Look sir, there she is!,' called out Crabb suddenly, pointing ahead of them to a red barge making its way further up the canal. 'And that looks like Mildred Chilton standing on the deck sir, with her back towards us.'

'Stop in the name of the law!' yelled Ravenscroft running up to the barge, as the startled man on deck quickly pushed the girl out of view down the hatch doorway.

'Stop this boat!' instructed Crabb.

'What the blazes!' said the man angrily.

'You are the *Grasshopper*?' asked a breathless Ravenscroft.

'What if we are? What's it to you?' retorted the man.

'My name is Inspector Ravenscroft. I have reason to believe that you have Mildred Chilton on board.'

'Mildred who?'

'Come my man, don't play the innocent with us,' said Crabb jumping onto the boat, closely followed by Ravenscroft and the constable.

'Here you, get off our boat,' said a fat, elderly, barge woman coming up the steps and brandishing a mop menacingly in Crabb's direction.

'Mildred Chilton. If you have harmed her in anyway, you will answer for it,' said Ravenscroft, as Crabb grabbed the mop end of the stick and began to wrestle it from the woman's grasp.

'You let go or I'll have your guts—' began the woman suddenly lunging to one side, losing her footing and crashing into the waters of the canal.

'My God look what you have gone and done now!' exclaimed the bargeman. 'I'll have you for this, peeler or no peeler.'

'Can your wife swim?' asked Ravenscroft looking down at the struggling woman.

'Course she bloody well can't swim! What do you think we are, frogs!'

'Then I suggest that you and my constable pull her out as quickly as possible,' instructed Ravenscroft.

The two men reached out for the struggling woman and began to pull her on board.

'Quickly Tom, while they are diverted, go below, and bring up the girl,' said Ravenscroft.

'What you gone and done that for?' moaned the bargeman rounding on Ravenscroft.

'Lost me footing, Bill,' spluttered the woman collapsing onto the deck. 'That young copper, he pushed me! 'Ere where's he gone?'

'My constable has gone below to bring up the girl. I am arresting you both for the kidnapping of Miss Mildred Chilton—' began Ravenscroft in a serious voice.

'It's not her, sir,' said Crabb interrupting his superior's words as he emerged on the deck followed by a young girl.

'What?' asked a startled Ravenscroft.

'It's not Mildred Chilton sir,' muttered Crabb.

'Then who — who is this girl?' asked Ravenscroft looking across at the young child.

'That's Alice, me granddaughter,' protested the woman spitting out a mouthful of water.

Ravenscroft stared at Crabb.

'What the devil do you mean by boarding my boat like this? I'll have the law on you!' exclaimed the man.

'We are the law,' replied Ravenscroft. 'Can you prove that this girl is your granddaughter?'

'Of course I can,' said the woman. 'Alice, tell them who you are, girl.'

'Alice Gazey sir,' said the girl in a quiet voice.

'There, what did I tell you?' said the man drawing himself up to his full height. 'Now what do you mean, sir, by attacking our boat like this and pushing my poor wife into the water?'

'Your wife slipped and fell into the canal; she was not pushed. And who are you sir?' inquired Ravenscroft trying not to look too embarrassed by the events of the previous few minutes.

'Henry Thomas Gazey, bargeman of these waters. My wife and I transport coal along the canals. A honest trade. We are on the way to Birmingham.'

'And why is this girl with you?'

'Her parents have gone away for a few days, so she is spending some time with us. There's nothing wrong with that is there?'

'Well Mr Gazey, my officers and I are searching for a young girl who has been cruelly abducted from her family in Droitwich. We received a telegram from the lock keeper here at Tardebigge, stating that he had seen a young girl on your boat matching the description of the missing girl. We naturally assumed that this missing girl was on your barge. I see now that we were incorrect in that assumption, and I would like to apologize for any inconvenience we may have caused you,' said Ravenscroft adopting a consolatory tone of voice.

'That's all very well. All very well indeed. It's easy for you to say that. Just look at my best pinafore. Ruined it is!' grumbled the woman rising to her feet and staring in Ravenscroft's direction.

'Of course. Perhaps this will recompense you for your inconvenience, and for the pinafore,' said Ravenscroft reaching into his waistcoat pocket and removing a coin which he passed over to the woman.

'That will do, I suppose,' replied the woman grudgingly accepting the coin.

'I wish you all good day. Mr Gazey,' said Ravenscroft jumping back onto day land, closely followed by Crabb and the policeman.

'And look next time before you come charging onto my barge!' shouted the man.

'Quickly, the sooner we are out of here, the better,' said a dejected Ravenscroft as the three men walked swiftly down the towpath to their waiting horse and trap.

* * *

'Confound that man, sending us that silly telegram,' said Ravenscroft with annoyance, sitting on a chair with his feet resting on the edge of the table, at the police station in Droitwich, later that afternoon.

'Never mind sir. It was worth a try. We had to follow it up,' replied Crabb trying to bring some light to his superior's darkened mood.

'I was sure that it was them. Everything seemed to fit: the time of their flight from Worcester; the young girl on the barge. Will we ever find Mildred Chilton and those awful Huddlestones or Drews? Confound it all, Tom!'

'We still don't know whether it was them that took young Miss Chilton.'

'You could be right,' answered Ravenscroft. 'Lucy certainly never saw the girl at that house in Worcester, but that does not mean that she wasn't there. She could have been upstairs, bound and gagged for all we know. What I don't understand is if they did take the girl, why did they feel the need to come back to Dodderhill to kill Old John? If he had seen them take the girl, he would not have known who they were, so there would have been no need to return and kill him. Some of this just does not add up.'

'What shall we do next, sir?' asked Crabb.

'If only I knew. If Mildred Chilton and her captors did not leave the town by either the canal or by road, and she is nowhere to be found in the immediate locality then . . .' began Ravenscroft. 'Tom, did anyone go to the railway station on that first day after Miss Chilton disappeared?'

'I think so sir. One of the men went, but I'm not sure.'

'What if that handkerchief was dropped into the canal to make us believe that Mildred and her abductor had left the town that way? What if they really left by train? How stupid we have been. Quickly Tom, the railway station!'

* * *

Ravenscroft and Crabb dismounted from the trap and made their way onto the station platform.

'The place looks deserted. There are clearly no trains expected in the near future,' said Ravenscroft.

'We could try the ticket-office,' suggested Crabb.

Ravenscroft walked across to the office. Finding the partition closed, the detective rapped on the glass.

Receiving no reply, Ravenscroft repeated his action. 'Where is the wretched man?' he said in an frustrated tone, all too aware that these enquiries, like all the others, might prove fruitless.

''Tis no good doing that sir. Won't do you no good at all.'

Ravenscroft turned round to find that the voice belonged to a tall, rotund, red cheeked man, who sported an untidy beard, and was dressed in a railway man's uniform.

'Next train to Birmingham is another hour yet.'

'So why is the ticket-office not open then?' enquired Ravenscroft.

'Folk don't usually arrive till ten minutes before train leaves. Ticket clerk is on his tea break,' replied the man stroking his beard. 'You'll have to come back then.'

'We are here on urgent business. Look my man, we are the law,' said Ravenscroft.

'Can see that. Your assistant has got on his uniform, so that means you'll be his superior officer then?'

'I am.'

'It's no matter. If you wants to go to Birmingham, you'll have to come back in fifty minutes, although I can't think why anyone would want to go there, smelly old place, all smoke and hot air—'

'We have no intention of travelling to Birmingham, or anywhere else for that matter,' interrupted Ravenscroft becoming annoyed by the station master's response.

'There's no need to get shirty with me, my good sir. No need for that, when a bit of common civility would not go amiss. If you don't want to go anywhere, then you shouldn't be here then should you? It is not my fault is it, if you don't know what you wants.'

'We want some information,' emphasized Ravenscroft, seeking to control his temper.

'Timetables are on the wall over there,' muttered the man turning away.

'Information about the missing girl.'

'What missing girl? I haven't heard nothing about no missing girl?'

'The girl that went missing last Tuesday afternoon,' said Crabb. 'The whole town knows about it.'

'Well I don't,' retorted the man.

'For goodness sake, man, where have you been the past four days?' asked Ravenscroft.

'Been down to Ross visiting me aunt. She is not well. Glad of the company. Only got back half an hour ago.'

'We are investigating the disappearance of Sir Charles Chilton's daughter. You have heard of Sir Charles?' asked Ravenscroft.

'Course I as. Lives at posh place on hill. Owns half the salt mines in Droitwich. Tetchy gent: the sort that's never satisfied with the answer you give them. I don't know why folks has to be so unpleasant,' replied the railway man shaking his head.

'Were you here on duty on Tuesday afternoon?'

'I was.'

'That was the afternoon Miss Mildred Chilton disappeared. She was abducted against her will. We have reason to believe that she, and the person, or persons, who took her, may have left the town by train. Can you remember seeing the girl? She is about eight or nine years of age, and would have been well dressed?' asked Ravenscroft hopefully.

'Young girl you say?' replied the man fingering his beard again. 'Can't say I . . . ah yes, young girl with that funny gent, about four o'clock in the afternoon.'

'Yes, go on,' encouraged Ravenscroft.

'Well there is nothing else to tell really. They sat on the bench over there. Quiet they were. Kept themselves to themselves.'

'A gentleman you say? Can you describe this gentleman for us?'

'Tall, thin, about forty I would say, wearing a shabby old suit and overcoat.'

'Had you ever seen this man before?' asked Crabb, making a note in his pocket book.

'No. Stranger to me he were.'

'And the girl, what was she doing?' asked Ravenscroft anxious to know more now that this new line of enquiry appeared to be bearing fruit.

'What do you mean — "doing"?' enquired the railway man.

'Well do you think the girl was being restrained, or held against her will in any way?' asked Ravenscroft.

'No. She just sat over there at the man's side. They were talking together. I did notice one unusual thing though. Man's eyes were everywhere.'

'How do you mean?'

'Well, his eyes were everywhere, looking one way and then the other, then at the girl, then looking at the rest of the folk on the platform. Those eyes, they had a funny look about them, dark, bit wild like, as though he were frightened of something. That's all I can tell you.'

'I see. That is most interesting,' replied Ravenscroft. 'I don't suppose you happen to remember where they were going to, this man and the girl?'

'Ticket clerk would know, but he's on his break. You'll have to wait until later. Afraid I cannot help you there sir.'

'Look, this girl may be in the gravest danger. We need to know where she was taken. I would be obliged if you would disturb your colleague as soon as possible and ask him to open this hatch,' urged Ravenscroft.

'Wait here, I'll see what I can do,' said the railway man walking a little way down the platform and entering the back of the ticket-office.

'We may be getting somewhere at last,' said Ravenscroft.

'Wonder who this man was?' asked Crabb.

Presently the glass partition of the ticket office opened.

'Ah, you must be the ticket clerk?' asked Ravenscroft.

'That's me,' replied the railway man.

'But, but, we spoke with you only a minute ago. We were under the impression that you were the station master,' said Ravenscroft somewhat taken back at seeing the same man again.

'Ah well, you thought wrong. I be the ticket clerk as well as the station master, but only on Tuesday and Friday afternoons. When I am the station master I cannot be the booking clerk, and when I'm the booking clerk I cannot be the station master. Can't do two jobs at once. It's against regulations.'

'But — we thought you were — oh, no matter. I would be obliged if you would come to the point.'

'Birmingham,' announced the railway man.

'Birmingham,' repeated Ravenscroft.

'That's what the gent said, one and a half single-third class tickets to Birmingham.'

'I see. You are sure they were single tickets?'

'You doubting my memory?'

'No of course not. It is just that we need to be sure where this man and the girl were going to. Well thank you for your time,' said Ravenscroft turning away.

'Paid for with a guinea.'

'I have no doubt. I wish you good day,' said Ravenscroft continuing to leave the station entrance.

'Wanted change he did.'

'Of course. Good day to you.'

'You ain't asked me about his hand,' called out the clerk.

'Hand? What hand?' asked Ravenscroft returning quickly to the hatch.

'Only three fingers and a thumb on his left hand. Saw it when he took his glove off to pay for his fare. Finger next to his small finger, gone, not there.'

'How very interesting. Three fingers you say? Thank you. There is nothing else you can tell us?'

'Nothing else,' said the railway man slamming the hatch closed with a bang.

'So, Tom, this is how Mildred and her abductor left the town that afternoon,' said Ravenscroft as he and Crabb made their way back to the horse and trap.

'At least we now have a description of him,' added Crabb.

'Yes, tall, middle aged man, with a wild look about his eyes, and a missing finger on his left hand. Interesting that he was talking to the girl. Mildred did not appear to be under any duress, according to the railway man. It suggests to me that she knew this man, and was quite willing to go with him on this journey. I find that very strange,' said Ravenscroft mounting the trap.

'Seems to rule out Mrs Drew.'

'Maybe. He could have been taking the girl to her, but then again Drew resided in Worcester, which is the opposite direction to Birmingham. Another thing I can't understand is if this man and the girl travelled to Birmingham, why did he then return to Droitwich to kill Old John?'

'Because he knew that Old John had seen him take the girl, and he was frightened that John would tell people who he was?' suggested Crabb.

'Exactly Tom! He wanted to make sure that Old John was out of the way. It still seems strange however that he would take the trouble to do that. He could have easily disappeared from view, with the girl, once they arrived in Birmingham. It is such a large place. However, I wonder whether they went there at all?'

'I don't understand sir?'

'Whoever took Mildred must have known that eventually we would make enquiries at the railway station, and if that wretched man had been on duty on Wednesday, we would have obtained this information earlier. The man who took Mildred would have known that we would make enquiries in Birmingham, perhaps without success, but once we had alerted the police stations there, they would have been on the look out for the couple. What if he went somewhere else instead, somewhere where we would never think of looking for him and the girl? He has tricked us once already, by leaving that handkerchief in the canal.'

'Like Worcester? Perhaps he was Mr Drew?'

'Doubtful. The neighbours never mentioned an adult male in the household. Right Tom, at least we now have a description of the man. I'll drop you off at the telegraph office. I want you to send a description of the couple to all the stations along this line, going in both directions. We must hope that some railwayman would have seen them alight from the train on Tuesday afternoon.'

'And what will you do sir?'

'I will return to Hill Court. I want to know who took Mildred, and why. Now that we have a description of the man, perhaps someone there will know who he is. We may yet find Mildred Chilton after all.'

* * *

'Good day to you sir,' said Jukes opening the main door for Ravenscroft.

'Good day again, Mr Jukes. I would like to see Sir Charles, if you would be so kind as to tell him I have arrived.'

'I'm afraid Sir Charles is not in at present sir. He is attending a business meeting in Bromsgrove. You have news of Miss Chilton?'

'We have not found Miss Chilton yet, but I have got a description of the man who took her,' replied Ravenscroft stepping into the hallway.

'That is good news, Inspector.'

'Tall, thin, about forty years of age, a wild look around the eyes, according to the station master at Droitwich station, with a finger missing from his left hand. Do you know of such a man?'

'No sir. I cannot recall anyone of that description. Missing a finger you say? No, I am afraid not. I will of course ask the other servants if they have seen anyone matching that description.'

'I would be obliged,' said Ravenscroft feeling somewhat deflated by the butler's reply. 'May I speak to Lady Chilton?'

'I am afraid not, sir. Lady Chilton is not well, and we have all been given strict instructions to admit no one into her presence. I am sorry sir. You may see Mr Brockway, should you wish. I believe he is in the study.'

'Then Mr Brockway it shall be,' sighed Ravenscroft.

'If you will come this way, sir.'

Jukes tapped on the door of the study and, receiving a reply from within, opened the door. 'Inspector Ravenscroft to see you sir.'

'Ah, Ravenscroft,' said Brockway rising from behind the desk and coming forward to meet the detective as he entered the room. 'I'm afraid Sir Charles is out at the moment. You have news of Miss Chilton?'

'We have yet to discover her whereabouts, but we now have a description of the man whom we believe abducted the young lady.'

'Indeed. That is progress indeed. Please take a seat, Inspector. That will be all, Jukes.'

'Miss Chilton was seen leaving the railway station in Droitwich on Tuesday afternoon. She was accompanied by a tall, middle aged man,' said Ravenscroft as Jukes left the room.

'I see,' said Brockway resuming his seat behind the desk.

'I wonder if you could place the man for us?'

'I will try, Inspector.'

'He was quite shabbily dressed, and was described as having a wild, haunted look about him.'

'I cannot recall such a person.'

'He was also missing a finger from his left hand,' continued Ravenscroft.

Brockway leaned back suddenly in his chair and covered the bottom part of his face with his hand.

'You know of such a man?' asked Ravenscroft eagerly.

'No. No. Missing a finger on his left hand? No, I know of no such man.'

'Forgive me, Mr Brockway, but you seem quite overcome?'

'It is the heat in here. This room often becomes warm in the late afternoon. I am always telling the servants to open the windows, but somehow they often seem to forget,' said Brockway rising from his chair, and walking quickly over to the window.

'Then you have never seen such a man? Perhaps Sir Charles has had dealings with such a man?' suggested Ravenscroft.

'I do not believe so, but I will mention this matter to Sir Charles upon his return, you may rest assured. Now if you will excuse me, Inspector, I have an urgent meeting to attend in Bromsgrove. Sir Charles will be expecting me to attend,' said Brockway crossing over to the door and opening it for the detective.

'Of course sir. I will not detain you longer,' said Ravenscroft rising from his seat and shaking the extended hand of the business man.

'Good day to you, Inspector.'

As Ravenscroft made his way down the corridor to the kitchens, he was now hopeful that his search for the missing girl would soon be over. He now had a description of the man who had taken her — but more importantly, he now knew that Brockway had lied to him.

CHAPTER TWELVE

DROITWICH

As Ravenscroft stood alone in the churchyard, he found his thoughts returning yet again, as they had done so many times earlier that day, to the house in Worcester and to the young girl whose remains he and Crabb had found beneath the stairs. Had the woman Drew killed the girl, or had she died of natural causes? The doctor had been unable to say one way or the other, but he felt that the former was the more likely. The fact that she had been buried so hastily under the stairs of that awful house strongly suggested that the Drew woman had been instrumental in her demise.

Then Ravenscroft remembered his own sister, Anne, she who had died suddenly at a similar age to the young girl, shortly before he himself had been born; the sister he had never known, but who had been remembered in their tiny household; the sister who had always been in his thoughts, and he knew would always be a part of his own life.

At least his own sister had been loved and cared for. The girl under the stairs had died a lonely death. Once she had been someone's child, perhaps even someone's sister. How, and why, had she ended her days in that dismal house in

Inkerman Street? How long had she been in the custody of strangers? Why had she been shut up and seldom seen by even the closest of neighbours? Questions that would perhaps remain unanswered, unless he could apprehend the Drew woman. She had been yet another unwanted child; whose poor mother had been forced to relinquish her, no doubt anxiously seeking to escape from penury or disgrace. She'd been farmed out for a few guineas to be forgotten for ever. And this last was the worst thing of all and the point which Ravenscroft found most difficult to accept — for the young girl who had been left behind, who had known no love, had no name, and had no other means of identification would, in her death, leave no remembrance for others to recall and mourn — the more he thought about her forlorn fate the angrier he became.

Now it seemed that Mildred Chilton had been taken by the same people and, unless Ravenscroft found her soon, he knew that she would in all probability meet the same fate as the poor unknown girl in Worcester.

He found his mind returning to the events of later in the day: the visit that he and Crabb had made to the railway station; how they had learnt that Mildred and her abductor had left the town that same afternoon, and the vivid description of her kidnapper he'd been given. At first he had been optimistic that someone at Hill Court would have been able to put a name to this man, but then as he questioned all the servants and labourers over the following two hours, he found that none of them had been able to place the stranger. He became increasingly depressed, and now as he watched the rain falling from the porch of the church, the lowering skies seemed to match his mood of deepening despair. And yet he knew that Brockway had lied to him. When he had given him the description of the man, Brockway had at first been visibly shaken, but had then quickly changed the subject and had been anxious to bring their conversation to a speedy conclusion.

If Brockway knew this man, then perhaps Sir Charles knew him as well? Perhaps the man had been someone they had previously done business with? But if this were the case, why had Brockway not acknowledged the identity of the man? Could it be that Brockway himself was behind the abduction of his employer's daughter? If so, what would have been the lawyer's motives? To extract money from Sir Charles, or was there some kind of personal revenge behind all this?

The servants had said that Sir Charles and Brockway would return before dark. All Ravenscroft had to do now was to wait upon their return, when he would confront the landowner and lawyer with the man's description.

Just who was this man? Apparently his appearance and manner had not frightened the girl. The railwayman had said that they had been talking quietly on the seat while they awaited the arrival of their train. Was he connected in some way with the Drew woman? After all, they had found the remains of that poor girl in Worcester, and she must have been the same age as Mildred Chilton. Perhaps the man was in the habit of kidnapping young girls and then selling them on to Drew? Was that how he earned his living? And yet, and yet, Brockway had known his identity, and Old John certainly had, and that was why he had been silenced — but how had he known him?

'I've come back for you, sir!'

He was startled by the sudden arrival of Crabb, who had darted into the porchway.

'Tom, how are you?'

'Bit wet, sir. They said at the house that you would be here,' replied Crabb brushing the rain away from his wet tunic.

'How did you get on, Tom?'

'I've sent out all the telegrams as you said, sir. Some replies have come back from the various station masters, but as yet no one can recall either the man or girl alighting from the train. Similarly in Worcester, the men have made extensive enquiries, but no one can recollect seeing the Drew woman and the others after they had left the house. They have even questioned the cab drivers again, but still no one can recall taking such a fare from the woman wanting to leave the city. She must have been met by someone, or perhaps they had their own transport. The woman just seems to have vanished into thin air. I just don't know what—'

'Stop, Tom! What was that you said?' said Ravenscroft suddenly.

'That the Drew woman must have vanished into thin air,' answered a puzzled Crabb.

'No, not that — when you first arrived here, just now?'

'Can't remember sir, something like, "I've come back for you".'

'"I've come back for you." That's what you said. Crabb, do you remember when we encountered Old John in this churchyard?'

'Lead us a merry dance he did, jumping from behind one tombstone to another.'

'Exactly, and do you remember that suddenly he pulled up short before one of the old vaults.'

'Looked as though he had seen a ghost,' added Crabb.

'Then he cried out — "He's come back for me! He's come back for me! He shan't take Old John."'

'Terrified he was.'

'Quickly Tom, do you remember which vault he stopped at?'

'That one over there, I think,' replied Crabb pointing at a large family vault lower down the path on the left hand side.

'I believe that was the one. Let's go and see who it belongs to, although I think I know the answer already,' said Ravenscroft leading the way out of the porch and into the rain.

The two men made their way down the path. Ravenscroft pulled some of the ivy away from one of the sides of the vault. 'Just as I thought Tom, it's the Chilton family vault. See here, Sir Christopher Chilton, the present Sir Charles's father, and yes, see round this side, Peter Chilton the elder brother who died so unexpectedly ten years ago.'

'But why was Old John afraid of an old vault like this?' asked Crabb through the pouring rain.

'He certainly knew both Sir Christopher and Peter Chilton. He had worked for both of them. When I spoke to Mrs Greenway in the kitchen garden, she said that Old John and Peter had been very close, going out riding together and such like, and that Old John had even brought back Peter's coffin from London with Sir Charles, for burial here.'

'Perhaps he was afraid of ghosts of the dead Chiltons; thought that one of them had come back for him, and that shortly it would be his time to join them?'

'And in that he was proved right. Within a day or so he was brutally murdered and had his corpse thrown into the canal. Perhaps the answer to this mystery has been here all the time? Let's get back in the dry, Tom.'

The two men ran back into the porch of the church.

'What I don't understand, is the fact that Old John spent most of his time in this churchyard, apparently he even slept here; he would hardly have done that if he had been afraid of ghosts. Then suddenly on the day we saw him, he runs all-round the churchyard, until he reaches the family vault where he becomes frightened out of his wits, before flying off as quickly as he could. I wonder why? I don't believe in ghosts, Tom,' said Ravenscroft wiping his wet spectacles on his handkerchief.

'They all said he was as mad as a March hare,' said Crabb.

'I think he had some kind of premonition that he was about to die,' suggested Ravenscroft deep in thought.

'It is probably not wise to give too much weight to what Old John said, and how he behaved.'

'You could be right, Tom. Anyway, enough of this damp porch. It will soon be dark. Let us go back to Hill Court and see if Sir Charles has returned yet? He and Brockway have some questions to answer.'

* * *

As Ravenscroft and Crabb ran towards the main door of Hill Court they became aware of a horse-drawn carriage standing near the entrance.

'It appears Sir Charles has returned,' said Ravenscroft walking up to the door and ringing the large bell pull.

'Good evening sir,' said Jukes opening the door.

'I see that Sir Charles is at home,' said Ravenscroft about to make his way through the entrance door.

'I'm afraid it is not convenient at the moment, sir,' said the butler barring his way.

'Who the devil is that, Jukes?' shouted a familiar voice from within.

'Inspector Ravenscroft, sir,' replied the butler, appearing ill at ease.

'Damn the man! Tell him to come back in the morning. It's damned inconvenient just now,' cried out the voice of Sir Charles Chilton.

'I'm sorry, sir. There is nothing more I can do. You must return in the morning,' said Jukes beginning to close the door.

'Whatever is that noise? I heard a disturbance inside,' protested Ravenscroft.

'It is nothing sir. One of the servants has upset the dinner, that is all.'

'Jukes! Tell Ravenscroft to come back in the morning!'

'I'm very sorry sir,' said Jukes abruptly closing the door in Ravenscroft's face.

'Well sir, that's a fine state of affairs. What on earth is going on inside?' said Crabb.

'Come Tom, let us leave as quickly as we can,' said Ravenscroft walking briskly away from the front entrance of the house and round to the side of the building.

'I could hear someone crying,' said Crabb following on behind.

Ravenscroft stopped quickly and looked around him in the thickening gloom. 'I think we are now unobserved. Follow me into those bushes.'

Crabb followed Ravenscroft into the undergrowth.

'Good, we won't be observed here. There's something going on in that house tonight. I have a feeling that someone is about to leave in that waiting carriage, and that Sir Charles does not want us here to witness the event,' said Ravenscroft hastily.

'What shall we do sir?'

'Well, Tom, if you do not mind this rain for a few more minutes, I think we will make our way back up here in this undergrowth, until we are able to observe what is about to take place.'

The two men made their way up the side of the garden, until Ravenscroft had a clear view of the carriage and the front door.

'This will do fine. Somehow I don't think we will have too long to wait,' said Ravenscroft.

Suddenly the front door was flung open, and a woman's voice could be clearly heard. 'No, no! You will not make me go!'

'That's Lady Chilton's voice if I am not mistaken,' whispered Ravenscroft.

'Not go! I shall not be brooked, woman! Staples, if you please, escort your patient, Lady Chilton, into the carriage,' said Sir Charles stepping out into the night air.

'I shall not go! I shall not go without Mildred,' retorted Lady Chilton appearing with Jukes and the doctor.

'Madam, it is the best for all concerned. Staples, have a care for your charge,' snapped Chilton.

'Sir Charles, I beg you to think again,' said an anxious Brockway joining the others.

'Do not cross me sir, if you value your position!' shouted Chilton. 'Staples!'

'Come, Lady Chilton. Calm yourself, my good lady. All will be well,' said Staples pushing a crying Lady Chilton into the waiting carriage.

'Please Sir Charles, this is not right,' pleaded Brockway. 'I ask you to reconsider man.'

'I pray you be silent, sir!' retorted Chilton slamming the door of the carriage behind the doctor and his patient. 'Away with you coachman!'

The man cracked his whip and the coach made a quick traverse of the circular lawn in front of the property, before disappearing from view down the drive. Sir Charles, Brockway and Jukes returned to the inside of the house, the latter closing the door behind them.

'Well sir, what was all that about?' asked Crabb.

'I don't know, Tom, but I do know that if we are quick we can collect our trap from outside the church, and we may then be in time to follow the carriage,' replied Ravenscroft making his way out of the undergrowth and walking quickly down the path towards the church.

The two men clambered into the trap; Tom cracked the whip and the horse set off at a brisk trot down the lane.

'Pull up the horse here,' instructed Ravenscroft. 'Let us hope that Sir Charles's carriage will be making its way down the main drive, and will come this way, rather than take the other direction towards Bromsgrove. I trust we are in time. I am anxious to see where they are taking Lady Chilton. Yes, there it is. Quickly Tom, follow on!'

Crabb cracked the whip once more, and the small trap turned the corner and followed the carriage as it made its way down the hill towards the town.

'We appear to be travelling out towards Worcester,' said Ravenscroft a few minutes later as the vehicles left the lights of the town. 'Not too close, Tom. We don't want to arouse suspicion. It is important that they do not know that they are being followed.'

'No fear of that sir. He's keeping up a good pace,' replied Crabb.

Their journey took them across the Heath and into the outer suburbs of Worcester.

'They must be taking her somewhere in Worcester,' said Ravenscroft straining to see in the wet, darkened streets of the city.

'We seem to be heading towards the cathedral, sir,' shouted Crabb through the rain.

'No, I think we are going across the bridge,' replied Ravenscroft. 'I guess that the cab's destination is nowhere here,' said Ravenscroft as the carriage continued on its way. 'I wonder where Staples and Lady Chilton are going to at this time? The poor woman clearly had no desire to go on such a journey at this late hour and in such conditions.'

A few minutes later the carriage suddenly turned left off the road, and disappeared from view down a long drive.

'Stop the horse here, Tom,' instructed Ravenscroft. 'Tie him up to that tree.'

The two men alighted from the trap and, after Crabb had secured the horse, they made their way towards the front gates to the driveway.

'See there, Tom,' said Ravenscroft pointing at the large range of buildings at the bottom of the drive. 'Quite an imposing residence. Fortunately some of the rooms are lit. We have often passed this place, and I have always wondered who owns it.'

'Shall we go and see who resides here?' asked Crabb.

'I don't think so at this time of night. Look, there is a brass plate affixed to the side of the gate post,' said Ravenscroft walking over to the sign. 'Perhaps this will give us some indication as to who the owner of this imposing residence is?'

'What does it say?' asked an eager Crabb.

'Good God!' exclaimed Ravenscroft. 'It says "Worcester Pauper and Lunatic Asylum". No wonder Lady Chilton did not wish to go to such a place!'

CHAPTER THIRTEEN

LEDBURY AND WORCESTER

'How absolutely dreadful,' said Lucy as she and her husband sat at the breakfast table in Ledbury the following morning. 'It sounds as though that terrible man has sent his wife to the lunatic asylum at Powick.'

'She could have been visiting someone there, I suppose,' replied Ravenscroft pouring himself another cup of tea. 'But somehow I don't think so. It was quite late at night, and she was certainly very reluctant to go there.'

'Does that awful man have the right to send his wife to that ghastly place?'

'He may have a good reason. By all accounts Lady Chilton has been ill for some time, and I certainly found her confused and melancholic when I spoke to her, but sending her for treatment to that place seems a bit drastic when she could be treated in her own home. Until just a few years ago, when a woman married a man, she and all her possessions more or less became his sole property, and he could do what he wanted to do with them, within reason of course.'

'Then it was a good thing that the law was changed,' replied Lucy indignantly.

'I do not make the laws, my dear, I only enforce them,' said Ravenscroft bringing the cup towards his lips.

'Well, what are you going to do about it?' continued Lucy in the same vein.

'Tom and I will visit the asylum today and see what is to be done. You may rest assured that I will do everything that I can to bring this case to a satisfactory conclusion, and see that Lady Chilton is restored to her family.'

'It sounds very much as though her husband does not want her. I would not have put it past him to kidnap his own daughter to cause his wife's breakdown.'

'That sounds a bit fanciful,' said Ravenscroft. 'And if he had arranged for his own daughter's abduction, where would he have hidden her?'

'Where do you think the poor girl is then?'

'I wish I knew. After we have been to the asylum, I intend having a word with Brockway. He may be the key to this whole business. I know he lied to me when I told him about the man who abducted Mildred Chilton.'

'Your mysterious man with only three fingers?'

'Yes. I am sure Brockway knows the identity of this man. He also seemed to be taking Lady Chilton's side last night. Perhaps he can also enlighten us on that matter as well.'

'I do hope you find the poor girl soon.'

'At least it would appear that she was not with that Drew/Huddlestone woman in Worcester,' said Ravenscroft taking another sip of tea.

'Unless she and the man with three fingers were working together? He could be holding her somewhere, before selling her on to Drew. It is quite terrible. I could not sleep all night for seeing that room again in Worcester. That poor boy, he looked so scared and afraid. And the baby. I am sure it was Miss Corbett's baby I could hear upstairs. I saw what looked like the baby's shawl downstairs. Then when you found the remains of that poor girl under the floor, it all became so awful," cried Lucy becoming increasingly agitated.

'Do not distress yourself, my dear. We do not know how the poor girl died, and it was obviously some time ago. At least we know that it was not Mildred Chilton. I am confident that she is still alive,' said Ravenscroft trying to sound reassuring.

'I do hope so. I wish the whole of this ghastly business was over with; that you had been able to find Mildred Chilton safe and well, and that I had been able to rescue those poor children.'

'You must not reproach yourself, my dear. It was very brave of you to enter that house on your own. Anything could have happened to you there. You should have let your Mr Shorter accompany you inside,' said Ravenscroft replacing his cup and wiping his lips on his napkin.

'That would only have aroused suspicion,' replied Lucy.

'Yes, I suppose you are right. Anyway, I must away. Time to collect Tom at the Wells and make our way to the asylum at Powick. I am sure that this will be the day that we finally reach the truth and reunite Mildred and her mother, and who knows we may yet find this Drew woman as well,' said Ravenscroft rising from the table and giving his wife a kiss. 'Take care my dear. I am sure all will soon be well.'

* * *

'Formidable, dreary old place,' muttered Crabb as the two men stood outside the front gates to the Worcester Pauper and Lunatic Asylum at Powick. The thick early morning mist still hung in the air, partially obscuring their view of the surrounding grounds, whilst adding to the intense stillness of the scene. Ravenscroft turned up the collar of his coat, seeking to protect himself from the cold damp, whilst Crabb uttered words of comfort to the horse as he secured the reins to a nearby tree.

The two detectives began to walk down the long driveway, passing a group of men who were busily digging a trench on one side of the grounds.

'Come on you men, put some heart into it,' shouted one of the figures who had the appearance of an overseer of some sort.

'Poor devils,' muttered Crabb. 'I should not like to be out here, digging away, on a morning like this.'

'No, I'm inclined to agree. Obviously those men have to earn their keep.'

'Rather them than me.'

'The place reminds me of a fortress. They clearly don't want people to come here in the first place and, once they are here — usually as the result of some misfortune that has befallen them — then they are not too enthusiastic about letting them go,' replied Ravenscroft as they reached the front door and he pulled the long wrought iron bell pull.

Some moments elapsed before the two men heard the sound of a large key being turned inside the old oak door.

'Visiting time is at four o'clock,' said an old woman partially opening the door.

'We are not here to visit any of the patients. My name is Detective Inspector Ravenscroft, and this is Constable Crabb. We would be obliged if we could speak with the Superintendent,' said Ravenscroft smiling.

'Superintendent is busy at present, you'll have to come back another day,' said the woman beginning to close the door.

'We are here on urgent business, which cannot possibly wait. It is of the utmost importance that I speak to your master concerning the admittance of one of your inmates,' said Ravenscroft firmly, whilst making sure that his boot had been placed into the partially opened space between the door and the frame.

'I'll see if he is available,' grumbled the woman, admitting the two men into the cold entrance hall, before shuffling down the corridor.

'I think I preferred it outside,' said Crabb looking around him at the stark interior.

'I agree it is not very welcoming, but then I suppose they get very few visitors here,' said Ravenscroft.

'No! No! Take it away!' shouted a voice somewhere in the distance, followed by a loud wayward laugh.

'My God, what was that?' said an alarmed Crabb.

'One of the inmates I would expect. Some years ago I had the misfortune to visit a similar establishment in London. I must say I did not particularly enjoy the experience, and was somewhat relieved when I left.'

'Come for Mary?' said a voice suddenly from behind Ravenscroft.

The two men turned to see an old woman dressed in a threadbare dress and tattered shawl standing behind them.

'You have come for Mary? Come to take Mary home?' continued the new arrival staring vacantly into Crabb's eyes.

'Sorry . . . I . . . don't . . .' began Crabb, taken aback by the new arrival.

'You like Mary? Come to take Mary away?' continued the old woman averting her gaze from Crabb to Ravenscroft.

'I am sorry, we are not empowered to assist you in any way,' replied Ravenscroft giving the woman a half smile.

'Why? You not like Mary? You take Mary away. She will look after you,' said the woman reaching out towards the detective.

'I cannot help you,' protested Ravenscroft as the woman placed her hands on his shoulders and stared close into his face.

'Take Mary away. You look a good man. Mary will give you a good time.'

'Come on now, miss,' said Crabb seeking to restrain the woman.

'You let go of me!' she retorted. 'You touch Mary and I will have your eyes out!'

'Be gone woman!' bellowed another voice. 'Get back to your room, Mary. These gentlemen have not come for you.'

Ravenscroft turned again to see a tall, rotund, middle aged gentleman, standing before them.

'Not come for Mary then? Not want Mary?' said the old woman staring wildly into Ravenscroft's eyes.

'Go away Mary before I send you to the laundry room!' shouted the new arrival.

'No! You not send Mary there?'

'Then take yourself off, woman,' instructed the man.

'Tomorrow you come for Mary. Come for Mary,' muttered the woman as she made her way down the corridor.

'Good morning, gentlemen. You must excuse the old woman. She has been here a very long time. She means no harm. I am Superintendent Woods. How can I help you?'

'We are given to understand that Lady Chilton was admitted to the asylum yesterday evening?' asked Ravenscroft coming straight to the point.

'I am afraid I cannot answer your question, Inspector. Information regarding our patients is entirely confidential.'

'I appreciate that, Superintendent Woods, but we are investigating a case of murder and childhood abduction in Droitwich, and believe that Lady Chilton may be able to assist us in our enquiries,' said Ravenscroft firmly.

'I will concede that Lady Chilton was admitted yesterday evening, but that is all I can tell you about her condition. You will have to see Sir Charles Chilton for more information, should he wish to disclose it,' replied the official, adopting what Ravenscroft regarded as a cold authoritative voice.

'We saw Sir Charles yesterday. He is fully informed about our activities,' lied Ravenscroft.

'I see, gentlemen.'

'Perhaps you would now tell us why Lady Chilton was admitted, and how long you expect her to stay with you?' asked Ravenscroft pressing home his advantage.

'Lady Chilton was admitted suffering from hysteria, a common complaint amongst ladies of a certain age, but then you would know that already if you have spoken to Sir Charles,' replied the superintendent casting a suspicious glance at Ravenscroft and Crabb.

'We believe that Doctor Staples is treating Lady Chilton?'

'That is correct, Inspector.'

'I would like to speak with the doctor.'

'I am afraid Doctor Staples is not here at present, although we do expect him later in the day, should you wish to return then.'

'Then I would like to see Lady Chilton—' began Ravenscroft.

'That is totally out of the question—'

'It is Lady Chilton's daughter who is missing. The situation is quite serious. The girl is in the gravest danger even as we speak. I believe that Lady Chilton may be able to provide us with vital information which may assist us in our search for the girl. I also believe that once Lady Chilton is reunited with her daughter, we will see a marked improvement in her condition. This is a situation with which Sir Charles would undoubtedly sympathize, and I am sure that he would be most generous towards you and your establishment for your assistance in this case,' said Ravenscroft in a quieter voice.

'I see, well—'

'And such a visit I am sure would not be incommodious to yourself. I assure you that our visit would be quite short, and that we would show the utmost discretion.'

'Yes, well, I suppose—'

'Thank you, my good sir. Then perhaps you would be kind enough to take us to see Lady Chilton?' smiled Ravenscroft.

'Yes, of course, gentlemen, if you would care to follow me.'

Ravenscroft and Crabb followed the superintendent up a long flight of stairs and along a drab, unappealing corridor. As they passed by the locked rooms the occasional sounds of crying, and shouting, could be heard from behind the closed doors.

'This is Lady Chilton's room,' said the superintendent stopping at one of the doors at the far end of the corridor, and placing the big iron key in the lock. 'We try to provide our guests with simple, but comfortable surroundings.'

'Thank you, superintendent. I wonder if we might see Lady Chilton alone? As she is known to us, I feel sure that she will be less distressed if she saw just my constable and myself, rather than seeing all three of us in the room.'

The official stared at Ravenscroft for a moment, then said, 'I will wait outside,' before opening the door.

Ravenscroft and Crabb entered the room, the latter closing the door behind them.

'Lady Chilton,' said Ravenscroft addressing the forlorn figure who sat on the chair facing the wall.

'Who are you?' asked the figure rising to her feet and coming forwards to meet the detectives. 'Has my husband sent you to take me home?'

'My name is Inspector Ravenscroft, Lady Chilton,' replied Ravenscroft in a quiet reassuring tone of voice. 'You may recall that we spoke, in your room, a few days ago.'

'Ravenscroft? Ravenscroft?' asked Lady Chilton looking vacantly at the two men. 'Why has my husband sent me here?'

'We are investigating the disappearance of your daughter, Mildred.'

'Mildred? Ravenscroft. Yes of course, you must forgive me,' said Lady Chilton giving a brief smile of recognition. 'You have found my daughter?'

'Not yet, ma'am,' said Crabb.

'But we hope to be successful within the next day or two. You may be able to help us Lady Chilton. We believe that your daughter was taken by a tall, thin, shabbily dressed man in middle-age. I wonder if you can recall seeing such a man recently.'

'No, I cannot help you.'

'The man is not perhaps one of your husband's business acquaintances?' continued Ravenscroft.

'No.'

'The man has a missing finger on his left hand,' said Ravenscroft hopefully.

'I know of no such man,' replied the other sadly.

'He is quite distinctive. You know of no one with a missing finger?'

'No. No. Why do you keep questioning me? I have told you that I do not know the man.'

'I am sorry,' said Ravenscroft, worried that he had caused alarm.

'Why has my husband sent me here? This dreadful place,' asked Lady Chilton a look of pleading in her eyes. 'You must take me away from here. I do not deserve this.'

'I do not have the authority to release you, Lady Chilton,' said Ravenscroft gently shaking his head.

'You must help me. I should not be held here!' exclaimed Lady Chilton reaching out and grasping Ravenscroft's coat. 'You must help me leave this place.'

'Please, Lady Chilton, do not distress yourself. I do not know why your husband has sent you here, but I know that all will be well quite soon, I can assure you. Please take a seat. Crabb, a glass of water if you will,' said Ravenscroft taking hold of Lady Chilton's arms and escorting her back to the chair.

Crabb looked around the uninviting room with its two chairs, bed, and washstand, and poured out a glass of water from the flagon that lay on the simple round bedside table.

'You must help me. Please help me find my daughter.'

'Drink this, Lady Chilton,' said Ravenscroft handing the glass to the distraught figure.

The woman looked at Ravenscroft for a few moments, before drinking the liquid.

'Lady Chilton, I realize that the situation in which you find yourself is quite distressing, but I give you my promise that I will find your daughter, and that when I have done so, you will be reunited with her, and that you will be released from this place,' said Ravenscroft calmly taking her hands, within his own, and looking directly into her eyes.

'You will find my daughter?'

'You have my word. All I ask is that you have faith that all will be well. I will return here within the next day or two. That is a firm promise. Be strong, Lady Chilton, for your daughter's sake. She will not want to see you distressed,' smiled Ravenscroft.

'Yes, yes,' responded Lady Chilton.

'I will return as soon as I have some news. Until then, my good lady, we will take our leave of you.'

As Ravenscroft and Crabb quietly left the room, Lady Chilton said nothing as she turned to face the window.

'Thank you,' said Ravenscroft as the superintendent turned the key in the door.

'If you will follow me gentlemen, I will see you out.'

'I will return in a day or so for Lady Chilton,' said Ravenscroft as they made their way back along the corridor.

'I am afraid I cannot release Lady Chilton without Sir Charles's permission.'

'Of course. I will bring such authority, you can be assured. Until then I would be obliged if you would take special care of the lady, and see that no harm befalls her, and that she has everything she wants,' said Ravenscroft taking a coin from his waistcoat pocket and handing it to Woods.

'Thank you sir. I can assure you that Lady Chilton will be well looked after.'

'Thank you. Tell me, Superintendent, are any of your patients permitted to leave the asylum of their own free will?' asked Ravenscroft as he began to descend the stairs.

'No sir. We take special care of our inmates here. It would not do for such people to roam freely. They can only be released if their condition improves, and only then with the authority of their doctors and relations. It is very rare that anyone leaves before their time.'

'Tell me, do any of your patients ever escape from the asylum?' asked Ravenscroft his curiosity aroused.

'Why do you ask, Inspector?' said the superintendent adopting a defensive posture.

'I was just curious to know. Has anyone left without your permission recently?' asked Ravenscroft.

'There was one gentleman. Name of Martin. He was out in the gardens planting some crops about a month ago. When the wardens counted up the numbers in the party at the end of the day, he was found to be missing.'

'I see. Could you describe this man Martin for us?' asked Ravenscroft stopping at the foot of the stairs.

'About forty years of age, tall, thin, of a docile personality.'

'Did he by any chance have a missing finger on his left hand?' asked Ravenscroft eagerly.

'Why yes. How did you know that, Inspector? Have you seen Martin? Have you got him in custody?'

'No, but I can tell you that this man Martin has been seen quite recently. In fact we believe that he is the man who has abducted Sir Charles Chilton's daughter.'

'Good heavens!' exclaimed Woods.

'What can you tell me about this man? It is a matter of great urgency.'

'I think you had better come into my office, gentlemen,' said the superintendent opening a door which led off the hallway.

'It is important that we learn as much as we can about this man,' repeated Ravenscroft as he and Crabb followed Woods into his room.

'I believe I may be able to supply you with some of the facts,' said Woods reaching for a large ledger on one of the shelves at the back of his desk. 'Yes, let me see. Martin. Martin. Ah, here we are. I cannot tell you a lot about him. It is just as I thought, he was already a patient at the asylum before I came here.'

'And how long have you been in charge here?' asked Ravenscroft anxious to know more.

'Just over six years.'

'And you say that this man Martin was already here when you came?'

'Yes. Ah, now this is interesting. Apparently four years ago Martin was undertaking some work in the kitchens, when he met with a serious accident. Something to do with one of the large knives. That must have been when he lost his finger,' said Woods looking down at the page of his ledger.

'Poor man!' exclaimed Crabb.

'Did Martin ever talk about Sir Charles Chilton or any other members of his family?' asked Ravenscroft.

'No. He was a man who kept very much to himself. He seldom spoke, and did not go out of his way to strike up any friendships with any of the other inmates.'

'I find it even more strange then that he should choose to escape and abduct Miss Chilton. Did he ever talk about leaving the asylum one day, and what he might do then?'

'No, as I said, he was a man of few words. Oh yes, there was one occasion when he had to be restrained.'

'When was that?'

'Shortly after he lost his finger, I believe.'

'Can you tell me the circumstances of what happened at that time?'

'I remember one of the wardens called me to his room. Martin was shouting, saying he had no reason to be here, and that he should be set free, and that he could stand it no more, or words to that affect.'

'What happened next?' asked Ravenscroft.

'We tried to reason with him, but to no avail. The man just fell to the floor, sobbing and crying, saying over and over again, that a great injustice had been done. We could do no more for him, so we left him alone in his room, making sure that all items of a harmful nature were removed. The next day, he was restored to his former self, and everything carried on as usual.'

'This is most interesting. Did you not believe this man Martin when he said he had been imprisoned here against his will?'

'Oh dear me Inspector, that is what a great number of our patients say,' laughed Woods. 'If we believed everything they told us, there would be no one here at all.'

'And just why was this man incarcerated here in the first place?'

'Let me see,' said Woods consulting the register once again. 'Here we are. The notes were made by my predecessor — "This man is a great danger both to himself and to society, and is not to be released under any circumstances", I think that answers your question Inspector.'

'Did no one ever question that statement?' asked Ravenscroft.

'No, we saw no reason to review the initial diagnosis. We could only do that if someone from the man's family urged us to do so.'

'And did anyone from his family do that?'

'As far as I know Martin appeared not to have any family.'

'So if he had not escaped last month, he would have been here for the rest of his life?'

'I suppose so.'

'Forgive me, Superintendent Woods, if I say that all that sounds rather harsh,' said Ravenscroft.

'It may appear so to you, Inspector, but you are an outsider. You do not know what these people have suffered in the past, and how society might be put at risk should they be allowed to go free once more. The fact that Martin has taken this girl would seem to support my view.'

'Tell me, Superintendent, did Martin ever mention anyone of the name of Huddlestone or Drew to you?' continued Ravenscroft, realizing that it would be pointless to pursue his argument, and hoping that a new line of enquiry would lead somewhere.

'No, I don't think so. The names are unfamiliar to me.'

'Well thank you, Superintendent, you have been most helpful. Rest assured that once we have found this man he will be returned to you. Oh, one more thing before we go — you mentioned that this man Martin had no family; did he ever receive any visitors at all?'

'No. No one.'

'You mean that no one was responsible for him?' asked Ravenscroft.

'No — oh yes, I see here that someone did call here once a year, and made a payment for his upkeep,' said Woods looking down at the page once more.

'Can you tell us the name of the person who made these payments?' asked Ravenscroft anxious to know more.

'Yes. The name is not entirely clear. Blackway, Brackway — no Brockway, I believe.'

'Brockway!' exclaimed Ravenscroft. 'Brockway. Now that is most interesting. You are sure, Superintendent, that the name is Brockway?'

'Yes, it comes back to me now. Once a year, Mr Brockway calls upon us, enquires about the health of Martin, and pays for his next year's upkeep.'

'Thank you, Mr Woods. Come, Crabb, we need to move quickly. I think I now know where Mildred Chilton can be found. It is time we rescued her.'

CHAPTER FOURTEEN

LEDBURY AND KIDDERMINSTER

Lucy stood by the window overlooking Church Lane, watching the raindrops making their slow, crooked way down the pane of glass; her thoughts returned once more to the small house in Inkerman Street, where she saw again in her mind's eye the stern, lined face of Mrs Huddlestone, and the forlorn eyes of the desperate young boy. She recalled her conversation there, and wondered what it was she had said to the woman that had so alarmed her, causing the occupants of the house to flee as soon as she had left.

Then there was the cry of the baby she was sure that she had heard, it seemed to come from the upstairs room, although the woman had denied this. The red shawl lying discarded in the corner of the room had confirmed her fears. Oh, how she had wanted to run up those stairs and recover the infant, and how she now cursed her indecision and lack of resolution!

In her dreams that night she had seen the boy cowering in the corner of the room, holding out the baby in his outstretched arms in her direction; tears of sorrow and longing ran down his face, entreating her to come to their aid. But as she had attempted to move towards the children, the dark presence of the woman had suddenly interceded between them, and she had found herself being pushed further and further away by this new darkened force. The increasing pain of her failure added to the desperate cries of the two children.

Despite the heat from the fireplace, and the confines of the small drawing-room, she felt a cold shiver run down her spine, as the awful realization swept over her that she might never see the boy again and that he and the infant might eventually suffer the same fate as the girl found under the stairs. And then there was Mildred Chilton. Why had she not be found in the house? Or had she also been confined to one of the upstairs rooms, held against her will, by that awful woman and her associates?

'Begging the intrusion, ma'am, but it's that strange man again, saying he must see you at all costs,' said the maid interrupting her thoughts.

'Mrs Ravenscroft, the day is saved! The Gorgon has been located in her den! Our prey is about to be netted! The veil is about to be lifted!' said Shorter rushing enthusiastically into the room and seizing Lucy's hands.

'Calm yourself, Mr Shorter,' said Lucy wondering what had caused such animation in the new arrival.

'Calm, Mrs Ravenscroft! This is not the time for calm. This is the time for decisions to be made! Time for us to act, my dear lady!'

'Whatever has happened?' asked Lucy.

'After the flight of our party, I decided to contact my fellow newspaper editors in the three adjacent counties, to see whether they had been approached to run similar advertisements in their journals. My esteemed colleague, Mr Nightingale of the Hereford Times remembered an advertisement which had been placed nearly a year ago in his newspaper, similar in content and language to the one which our Mrs Huddlestone placed in my own paper.'

'Hereford. So that is where they have gone,' interjected Lucy breaking into the fast flowing words of the newspaperman.

'Not so. Ah, it's cunning my dear lady — very cunning. Our Mrs Drew is sly!'

'Whatever do you mean?'

'Although the advertisement had been placed in the Hereford Times, the box address was given as a Mrs Polly Huddlestone residing in Kidderminster no less!'

'Kidderminster — but why Kidderminster when the advertisement was placed in the Hereford newspaper?' asked Lucy.

'That is where the cunning comes in, my dear lady. By placing an advertisement for an unwanted child in one town, and having the address in another, the Drew/Huddlestone woman was hiding her tracks. Extremely clever. Could not have thought of it myself. We are dealing with a very ingenious and dangerous person. The deception of the woman!'

'I see. I remember my husband saying that he had been told by the next-door neighbour that there was a daughter, called Polly, who used to call on them.'

'There you have it!'

'So that is where the Drew woman has gone — to her daughter's in Kidderminster.'

'Exactly!'

'Mr Shorter, you are so wonderful. How clever of you to have thought of contacting your fellow newspaper editors.'

'It is nothing, my dear lady. We newspapermen are used to making investigations in our quest for the truth. No stone is left unturned by the seekers of knowledge. If the pan is cold and empty, then you must look for other food to fill it, as they say.'

'We must travel to Kidderminster at once,' said Lucy eagerly.

'My own sentiments exactly, my dear Mrs Ravenscroft, but perhaps it would be advisable if we were to inform your husband first?'

'I'm afraid my husband is away at present.'

'Ah yes, the Droitwich disappearance. Quite understand. "Constabulary duty to be done." Then perhaps we should visit the police station in Kidderminster and engage their assistance, before we seek out the Drew woman?'

'I think that might be wise,' said Lucy hastily writing a note to leave for her husband, and then calling her maid.

'There is a train in fifteen minutes. We can be there within the hour,' said Shorter excitedly. 'What a story all this will make! The pen is poised, my dear Mrs Ravenscroft. The pen is ready!'

* * *

Later that morning, Lucy and Shorter, accompanied by a uniformed police officer, made their way down the narrow alleyway that ran between the two rows of brick houses, that lead away from the police station, in the town of Kidderminster.

'Number thirty-five, ma'am,' pronounced the constable. 'What would you like me to do, Mrs Ravenscroft?'

'I will knock on the door first,' said Lucy.

'What a miserable looking place,' muttered Shorter looking at the shabbily constructed terraced house.

'Ready when you are, ma'am,' announced the officer.

'Good luck, my dear lady,' said Shorter giving an encouraging smile.

Lucy returned the smile, then moved towards the house. On the journey to Kidderminster, as they had sat together on the train, watching the stations of Malvern, Worcester and Droitwich pass by slowly, it had seemed as though their journey would have no end, and as they had walked down the hill into the centre of the town, doubts began to enter her mind. What if the address they had been given did not exist? What if the Drews had lived there before their stay in Worcester and had now moved elsewhere? What if she arrived too late and some terrible misfortune had befallen the children? Now all those questions were about to be answered — and she hoped against hope that they had not come too late.

There had been no sign of movement from inside the house, no signs of moving curtains or eyes observing her arrival. As she raised her shaking gloved hand and bought it down on the woodwork, she felt a cold anxiety within her taking hold, and prayed that she would keep her nerve in what was about to follow.

Receiving no reply, she strained to hear any possible noise from within the house, she repeated her action, but again there was no response.

So, they had left. She was too late.

'Let me try, ma'am,' said the officer joining her. 'Open up. Police!' he shouted, banging his fist heavily on the door. 'Open up in the name of the law!'

'They have gone,' said Lucy sadly.

'Stand back, ma'am,' indicated the policeman, taking three steps backwards then rushing at the door.

The wood gave way.

'Best if I go first, ma'am,' said the constable entering the building.

Lucy and Shorter followed.

''Ere what are you doing!' exclaimed a voice from within.

'We believe a Polly Drew lives here,' said the constable addressing the old woman, whom Lucy recognized as Granny Thomson.

'What she doing here?' said the woman pointing angrily at Lucy.

'Where is Mrs Drew?' asked Lucy anxiously. 'Where are the children?'

The woman said nothing as she shrugged her shoulders and turned away.

'I'll look upstairs, Mrs Ravenscroft,' said the Constable.

'I'll look in the backroom,' said Shorter.

'Where are the children?' repeated Lucy. 'For God's sake tell me where the children are.'

The old woman gave her a surly look, before seating herself at the table.

'No one upstairs, ma'am,' said the constable returning to the room.

'There seems to be no one in the backroom either,' said Shorter.

'Please tell me where they are. Where are the children? What have you done with Mildred Chilton?' implored Lucy, feeling that her heart was about to break.

'Who is she? I don't know anybody of that name,' said the old woman.

'The birds must have flown the nest,' said a dejected Shorter.

'If you have one ounce of humanity in you, tell me where the children are?' said Lucy.

The old woman looked away and remained silent.

'Oh, Mr Shorter, we are too late!' cried out Lucy. 'They have evaded us again.'

'Do not distress yourself, my dear lady,' offered Shorter.

'Why is it that they are always one step ahead of us?'

'They cannot run for ever.'

'What is that noise?' said Lucy suddenly.

'What noise, ma'am?' asked the constable.

'I'm sure I heard a noise. Tapping. Somewhere in this room. Cannot you hear the noise? Over there!' exclaimed Lucy pointing at the blue painted cupboard situated in the corner under the stairs.

The constable sprang forwards and opened the door.

'Please don't hit me! I ain't done nothing wrong,' said a voice from within.

'It's the boy! Let me speak to him,' said Lucy kneeling down by the cupboard.

'The old woman must have locked him inside when she heard us,' remarked Shorter.

'Do not be afraid. We will not harm you. You remember me. I came the other day to the house in Worcester. Give me your hand,' said Lucy reaching out slowly for the boy.

'Don't want to come out. She will hit me.'

'It's all right. Mrs Drew is not here. You are safe now.'

The boy hesitantly accepted Lucy's hand and stepped out of the cupboard. 'You going to hit me?'

'No, of course not,' said Lucy clasping the ragged child tightly to her, seeking to bring comfort to the sobbing figure. 'There is nothing to fear. We have come to save you.'

'Poor child,' said Shorter stepping forward.

The child, alarmed by the sudden movement of the newspaperman, broke free of Lucy and moved quickly to the side of the room, where he sank to his knees and sought to cover his face.

'It's all right. These gentlemen are with me. They mean you no harm. Give me your hand,' said Lucy reaching out again for the child. 'What is your name?'

'Harold,' said the boy dragging his arm across his tear-stained face.

'Well Harold, how old are you?' asked Lucy smiling and looking into the child's face.

'Don't know,' came back the answer.

'Never mind. Would you like a drink?'

The boy nodded.

'Constable, perhaps you could see if there is any water in the kitchen. Now Harold, take a seat here by me at the table. Don't worry, Granny Thomson can't harm you now. She will never harm you again.'

The old woman gave the child a brief stare, then made her way out into the back kitchen.

The constable returned bearing a broken cup which he placed on the table. The boy reached out for the vessel and quickly consumed the water.

'Lad must have been thirsty,' remarked Shorter. 'Looks as though he could do with a good meal or two.'

'Can you tell me where Mildred is?' asked Lucy.

The boy said nothing as he stared vacantly into Lucy's face.

'Mildred Chilton? The young girl who was taken several days ago. You remember Mildred?'

'Girl?'

'Yes. Mildred,' urged Lucy.

'There was a girl. She's dead.'

172

'Oh my God!' exclaimed Lucy. 'Mildred is dead! We have come to late!'

'Under the stairs, girl is under the stairs,' muttered the boy.

'I believe, Mrs Ravenscroft, that the boy is referring to the girl who was buried some time ago under the stairs in Worcester,' suggested Shorter.

'When was this girl buried?' asked Lucy.

'Don't know. Many weeks ago. Just after I came.'

'Then Mildred must still be alive, thank God! Can you tell me where the girl is now? Where is Mildred,' pleaded Lucy.

The boy said nothing as he looked down at the floor.

'Harold, can you tell me where Mrs Drew and the baby are?' asked Lucy, changing her line of questioning, and placing her hand on the child's arm.

'Don't know.'

'Were they here in the house, just now, before we came?'

The boy nodded and took another drink from the replenished cup.

'Then they left the house?'

'Yes.'

'Who went out from the house?' asked Lucy. 'Mrs Drew?'

The boy nodded again.

'And the baby? Did he go with her?'

'In pram. Babby went out.'

'She has taken the baby. We must go after them,' said Lucy addressing Shorter.

'We don't know where they have gone,' replied the newspaperman. 'Perhaps they may return in a few minutes. If we were to wait for them, all may not yet be lost.'

'Gone to canal,' interrupted the boy. 'Going away. Not coming back. Like other one.'

'Like which other one?' asked Lucy anxiously.

'Babby. He not come back,' replied the boy staring into his benefactor's eyes.

173

'Oh my God!' exclaimed Lucy. 'She means to drown the baby!'

'Begging your pardon ma'am, but you don't know that,' said the policeman.

'Where is the canal?'

'Turn left at the end of the road and follow it down to the bottom of the hill,' replied the constable.

'We must be quick. Mr Shorter, will you come with me?' asked an agitated Lucy. 'Of course, my dear Mrs Ravenscroft.'

'Constable, will you look after the boy until we return.'

'Certainly, ma'am.'

'Quickly, Mr Shorter. I fear she intends to drown the baby. Pray God we will be in time to prevent her!' said Lucy running out of the house, closely followed by Shorter.

Reaching the corner of the road, Lucy paused for a moment.

'This way, my dear lady,' indicated Shorter.

They ran quickly down the cobbled street.

'There is the canal,' shouted a breathless Shorter pointing ahead of him.

'We must save the child!' said Lucy fearing the worst.

A few hundred yards bought them to the water's edge.

'Oh my God! I can't see them,' cried Lucy frantically looking all around her. 'Which way have they gone?'

'Over there!' shouted Shorter. 'In the distance. See that figure. That could be the woman.'

'Quickly Mr Shorter, we must reach them,' said Lucy running along the towpath of the canal. 'It is her, I'm sure. See, she is pushing a perambulator. Pray God we are in time!'

As they approached the figure, it seemed to Lucy that it turned, looked hesitantly in their direction, before quickening its pace.

'Stop!' shouted Lucy attempting to run faster. 'We must not let her get away. She has the child.'

'Fear not, my dear lady, she is no match for us,' gasped Shorter.

Suddenly the figure stopped and turned to face them. Dressed in a black coat, shawl and bonnet, Lucy recognized her as Mrs Drew.

'You!' exclaimed the woman. 'You came to my house in Worcester. Deceitful little hussy with your fancy tale. You sought to entrap me. What do you want with me?'

'Give me the child,' demanded Lucy.

'Not yours to have, my dear,' replied Mrs Drew in mocking tone.

'We have found the boy,' said a breathless Shorter. 'He is safe from your clutches.'

'The boy is mine. You have no right. Just as this baby is mine. Given to me by his parents for me to look after,' said the woman adopting a lofty tone.

'We know what you do,' protested Lucy.

'And what is that, my dear?'

'You're a common criminal. You take payments from vulnerable young mothers in exchange for their children.'

'And what if I do? That is a good Christian thing to do, is it not?'

'What happened to the other baby?' asked Lucy. 'What have you done with the other baby?'

'What other baby?'

'The child given to you by Miss Belinda Parkes, the housemaid in Droitwich,' said Shorter recovering his breath.

'Died, my dear. It was sickly. I did all I could for it, but the good Lord chose to take her away from us,' smiled Drew.

'What about the girl who died in Worcester?' asked Lucy.

'I'm sure I don't know what you are talking about, my dear.'

'The girl whose body my husband found under the stairs,' said Lucy feeling the desperation in her own voice.

'I know nothing about the girl,' said the woman defiantly. 'Now if you will excuse me.'

'Where is Mildred Chilton? What have you done with her?' asked Lucy.

'Don't know what you're talking about,' repeated Drew.

'Where is Mildred Chilton?' repeated Lucy.

'Madam, I urge you to give up that child,' demanded Shorter.

'By what authority do you speak?' sneered the other.

'The police, ma'am. I speak on behalf of the police,' replied Shorter forcefully.

'You lie!' retorted Drew.

'I suggest you hand over the child, or you will answer for your crimes, to our readers, inside the pages of the Droitwich Guardian!' said Shorter drawing himself up to his full height.

'I have nothing to fear from you, you little newspaper-man, and your silly newspaper,' laughed Drew.

'If you have nothing to fear, return with us now to the police station,' implored Lucy taking a step forwards.

'Keep away! I warn you to keep away!' shouted the woman.

'Give me the child. She has done you no harm. Her mother is waiting for her. I beg you,' said Lucy tears beginning to well up in her eyes.

'I warn you, keep away!' said Drew pushing the perambulator to the edge of the path, and balancing its front wheels over the edge of the waters.

'No!' shouted Lucy. 'For God's sake have mercy!'

'Mercy! You ask for mercy,' taunted Drew.

'Not for me. For the child,' cried Lucy. 'Give us the child.'

'For pity's sake, woman,' said Shorter moving closer to the woman and the pram.

'If you want the child, then you shall have her,' laughed the woman as she thrust the perambulator over the edge of the path.

'Oh, my God!' exclaimed Lucy as the black vehicle began to sink into the muddy water. 'The child!'

'Fear not my good lady,' said Shorter quickly discarding his coat and glasses, and throwing them onto the ground, before plunging into the murky waters of the canal.

Lucy let out a desperate cry as first the perambulator disappeared from view, and then this was closely followed by the journalist.

'Oh my God! Please save them!' shouted Lucy noticing that a group of men were running along the towpath in her direction.

'I have her!' spluttered Shorter suddenly emerging from the water and holding up a bundle. 'I have her!'

'Well done, Mr Shorter. Make your way over to the side and pass me the child,' instructed Lucy kneeling down on the path and stretching out her hands.

Shorter passed over the bundle.

'I pray God we are not too late,' said Lucy laying the bundle on the side of the path and quickly turning back the wet shawl.

'You all right, squire?' asked one of the men rushing to the side of the bank and pulling out a sodden Shorter.

'The child. It is the child, I recognize the red shawl!' cried out Lucy.

'Are we in time?' asked a gasping soaked Shorter.

'Please God, let it be alive,' said a frantic Lucy pulling back the tightly bound wet outer layers of the bundle.

'Can I help you, ma'am?' asked one of the men.

'I see her face. She does not appear to be breathing. No, no!' cried out Lucy drawing the child to her and frantically rubbing its back. 'Please, please, let the baby live!'

Suddenly the child let out a loud cry.

'Praise be!' exclaimed a relieved Shorter. 'It's alive!'

'Oh, Mr Shorter, we were just in time,' said Lucy tears of joy flowing down her face.

'Capital. Capital, my dear lady,' said a smiling Shorter laying a wet hand on Lucy's shoulder and peering over at the crying child.

'She must be very cold. We must take her indoors as soon as possible. I thank God that we were just in time. Thank you, Mr Shorter. Thank you.'

'All in a day's work my dear Mrs Ravenscroft. This will make fine copy. What a story to tell all our readers. We have had nothing like this for years in the Droitwich Guardian. Such excitement! Such endeavour!' said an excited Shorter looking around for his discarded spectacles.

'Indeed, Mr Shorter. Where is that awful woman?' asked Lucy. 'Where has she gone?'

Shorter looked all around him. 'I fear our Mrs Drew has taken advantage of our inattention to secure her own disappearance. The bird has flown from the soiled nest. Alas, the condemned woman has escaped the hangman! She is nowhere to be seen!'

'Then where is Mildred Chilton?'

CHAPTER FIFTEEN

DROITWICH

'Good day, Sir Charles,' said Ravenscroft, as he and Crabb entered the study of Hill Court later that morning. 'I trust you will have no objection if Mr Russell and Miss Petterson join us as well?'

'I have the greatest objection, my dear sir. That man is not welcome in my house,' retorted the landowner eyeing the younger man.

'I can assure you, Sir Charles, that I have no desire to be here either, but Inspector Ravenscroft was most insistent that I should be present,' said Russell casting a fleeting sideways glance in the governess's direction.

'What the deuce is this all about, Ravenscroft? I still cannot see why these individuals need to be present,' growled Sir Charles.

'It is about your daughter, sir. I believe that each one of us may have important information. If we are to secure the release of Miss Chilton it is important that we are all present for this discussion today. I believe we are very close to securing your daughter's release from her captor,' said Ravenscroft in a forthright manner.

'Oh very well then,' said a reluctant Chilton seating himself behind his desk. 'I must insist however that Brockway remains here.'

'Of course, Sir Charles. In fact I think it is most crucial to our deliberations that Mr Brockway be present,' said Ravenscroft looking across at the lawyer, who turned quickly away. 'And I would be obliged if Mr Jukes would remain also.'

'Yes sir,' replied the butler looking somewhat confused.

'Well get on with it, man. I have an important meeting to attend in Birmingham later today,' said Chilton lighting one of his cigars and blowing the smoke out into the room.

Russell and the governess seated themselves together on the sofa, whilst Crabb and the butler stood by the door.

'Since we began our investigations into the abduction of Mildred Chilton, we have been cruelly deceived by most of you here today,' began Ravenscroft, realizing that if he were about to unravel the truth he would need to proceed with care and attention. 'Miss Petterson lied to us when she stated under questioning, that she had only entered the church for only five minutes to see which hymns had been chosen for Sunday service. You, Mr Russell, lied to us when you declared that you had not visited the church on that day, when in fact both of you had been meeting there in secret for several weeks.'

'Had they, by God!' exclaimed Sir Charles. 'This is interesting, Ravenscroft. Carrying on under my very nose, were they! We will soon have an end to that.'

'Miss Petterson is now in my protection,' said Russell placing his hand on the lady's arm.

'It's as well she is, sir, because she is in no way welcome here anymore,' replied Chilton, as the governess looked down at the floor.

'Then there is you, Mr Brockway. You lied to me when you said you did not recognize the man who was seen at the railway station with Miss Chilton,' continued Ravenscroft.

'I have told you I do not know the man,' protested the lawyer avoiding Ravenscroft's stare.

'And you, Sir Charles, have deceived us the most, as will be made plain presently.'

Chilton said nothing as he looked down at some papers on his desk.

'Let us begin by examining the events of the day that Miss Chilton went missing. You, Miss Petterson, took your charge to the churchyard and entered the church where your lover, Mr Russell was waiting. You remained in the church for approximately fifteen minutes, plenty of time for Miss Chilton to be abducted by the man with three fingers. At first it would appear that she had been taken against her will, but the station master at the station saw no forced abduction, only two persons talking quietly together on the platform.

'I believe that Miss Chilton knew the person who took her, because they had spoken before that day, in that church-yard, and on at least one other occasion, when you, Miss Petterson, and you Mr Russell, had kept your weekly rendezvous in the church. Mildred was not abducted, she went willingly. We then have to ask ourselves why did she go with this man — and who was he?'

'This is all very interesting, Ravenscroft, but is it getting us anywhere?' protested Sir Charles leaning back in his chair and blowing out more smoke into the room.

'Let us now turn to the identity of this man, for he is the key to the entire mystery. When I described the man to the servants and to other local people no one could identify him a man with three fingers; only you, Mr Brockway, clearly knew his identity. When I visited the asylum in Worcester earlier today I learnt of a man called Martin—'

'You what, sir!' interjected Chilton.

'Please let me continue,' said Ravenscroft firmly. 'This man Martin had been in the asylum for at least six years, and probably for much longer than that, for so long in fact that everyone had quite forgotten about him. Three years ago he lost a finger in an accident in the kitchens. That was why no one here could identify him, because his injury had been a recent one. However you, Mr Brockway, knew of the man's injury because you visited the asylum each year to make payments for Martin's upkeep, and it was on one of these visits that you learnt of this accident. Is that not so, Mr Brockway?'

'Say nothing, Brockway, the man does not know what he is talking about,' said Chilton, as the lawyer sighed and looked downcast.

'There was of course one other person who witnessed the abduction of Miss Chilton, and that was Old John. He was in the churchyard that day, and saw the couple meet and leave together. Furthermore he recognized the man and that of course was why he was silenced. Now let us turn to the events of ten years ago.'

'What on earth for?' protested Chilton. 'What have the events of ten years ago to do with the disappearance of my daughter? She had not even been born then.'

'That was when your brother Peter died quite suddenly I believe, on a business trip to London,' continued Ravenscroft ignoring Chilton's protestations.

'Yes, and we buried him in the churchyard here at Dodderhill.'

'That is what everyone thought at the time. After all, had not you Sir Charles, and Old John travelled to London when you heard the news, and did you not both bring back the body for burial here?'

'Yes, yes, but where is all this leading?' asked Sir Charles impatiently.

'Then you would not object if I applied for an exhumation order to open up the tomb and examine the body?'

'The deuce you will!' protested Chilton.

'Oh, I think you will find that I have the authority to order such an exhumation, Sir Charles. Of course I would not expect your brother's body to be there. In fact Peter Chilton is very much alive. For the past ten years he has been locked away in the asylum at Worcester, or he was until a month ago, when he escaped. You see, your brother Peter Chilton, and Martin — the three fingered man — are the same person!' said Ravenscroft pausing for effect.

'Master Peter alive!' exclaimed Jukes.

'This is all nonsense, Ravenscroft. Pure conjecture. My brother died ten years ago. I buried him myself,' declared Chilton.

'I do not think so. Certainly the burial service took place. I have no doubt of that. The church records state as much.'

'Well there you are then,' pronounced Chilton.

'But I believe that the coffin you buried was empty. I believe that you were profoundly jealous of your brother, Sir Charles. After all he stood to inherit the family business, besides being engaged to an attractive woman, whom you no doubt desired, whereas you stood to gain nothing once your father had died. So a plan was formulated. You and Old John overcame your brother, when he was away from home, and had him incarcerated in the asylum, no doubt telling the authorities there that your brother was mad, and that he was not to be released under any circumstances. I am sure that he tried to tell his keepers there that a gross mistake had taken place, but they of course took no notice, believing him to be deranged—Or were they paid to make sure that he did not escape? The years went by. The payments continued to ensure that he would never be released. They even gave him a new name — Martin, in an attempt to take away his previous identity,' continued Ravenscroft anxious to press home his advantage.

'Pure fantasy!' protested Chilton. 'This is all nonsense!'

'When you had safely secured your brother in the asylum, you told everyone that Peter had died. You and Old John bought back the weighted coffin, making everyone believe that Peter had died quite suddenly of a fever in London — and so you buried him in the churchyard. Then you had to get rid of Old John, as he knew too much. Whilst John was still a hired hand here there remained the possibility that one day he would talk too much and tell others what had really happened, and so you dismissed him from your employment. Old John was half mad anyway, and if he did tell anyone the truth, it would be doubtful that he would have been believed. People would have just dismissed such ramblings, believing that an embittered man was merely trying to get his own back. And then of course you were free to inherit the family salt business, when your father died shortly afterwards, and you were also free to marry the woman who had been betrothed to your brother.'

'This is all utter nonsense — pure fabrication!' scoffed Chilton. 'Take it to a court of law, sir, and see how far you will get. I will see that you are ruined, Ravenscroft, if you insist on continuing with this nonsense.'

'Is it really all fabrication as you claim, Sir Charles? Here is the exhumation order,' said Ravenscroft taking out a sheet of paper from his coat pocket and holding it aloft. 'Shall we now see who is telling the truth?'

'For goodness sake, Sir Charles, tell them the truth—' began the lawyer.

'Be quiet, Brockway!' threatened Chilton. 'Have a care sir, if you value your position.'

'Ah Sir Charles, this is the man you sent to the asylum every year, to pay the authorities enough money to ensure your brother would never be released!' exclaimed Ravenscroft waving the paper. 'And now you have sent your poor wife to the asylum. I wonder why? Has she suddenly learnt the truth after all these years, that you falsely imprisoned the man she once loved? Is that why she has been taken to that awful place, where she can speak to no one and where she will be ignored for the remainder of her days?'

'Get out of my house, Ravenscroft, before I call the servants!' said an indignant Sir Charles stubbing out his cigar and rising from his chair.

'For goodness sake, Charles, tell them the truth,' called out Brockway. 'We cannot go on like this.'

'Have a care, sir, I repeat again, have a care, if you wish to remain in my employ,' sneered Chilton turning on the lawyer.

'I will not be silenced anymore. It is all true, Inspector, every word of it. Sir Charles imprisoned his brother in the asylum, and I was sent there every year to make the payments to see that he did not leave. And now he has sought to imprison poor Lady Chilton. I cannot remain silent. I will not stand idly by why you continue with these outrages,' said Brockway confronting his employer.

'You will confirm all this, Mr Brockway, in a court of law?' asked Ravenscroft realizing that the advantage was now his.

'You have my assurance of that, sir,' said Brockway.

'Damn you sir, damn you!' muttered Chilton as he sank back into his chair.

'Thank you, Mr Brockway. I appreciate that you were an unwilling partner in this business,' said Ravenscroft.

'Forgive me, Inspector, but none of this helps us to find Mildred,' said Miss Petterson.

'On the contrary it helps us a great deal, for once I had learnt that Martin and Peter Chilton were one and the same, I knew where Miss Chilton could be found.'

'How? I don't understand,' said Russell.

'It was Mrs Greenway who provided me with that answer.'

'Mrs Greenway, sir?' asked a startled Jukes.

'Yes, Mrs Greenway, the cook. That morning when we met in the garden, she told me that Master Peter had been close to his old nanny, Nanny Jones, who had retired many years ago to her cottage in the nearby village of Elmbridge. When Peter escaped from the asylum he had to go somewhere. He could not return here, for he knew that he would be taken back to the asylum, but he remembered his old nurse, Nanny Jones, and made his way there. No doubt the old woman was delighted to see him. Peter then learnt that his brother had married the woman he loved, and had taken over the business, and so he decided that he would seek his revenge by abducting Mildred. He may also have believed that Mildred was perhaps his own daughter. He came back to Dodderhill, and watched and waited until the time was ripe. He discovered the liaison between you, Miss Petterson, and you Mr Russell, and your clandestine meetings in the church, and introduced himself to Mildred, gradually establishing a relationship with the girl, and no doubt telling her that he was really her father, and swearing her to secrecy.

'They arranged to go away together and so they met again on that fateful afternoon when they left the churchyard together. On the way to the railway station, Peter dropped Mildred's handkerchief in the canal, to make us believe that they had left the town on one of the canal boats. He purchased two single tickets for Birmingham, hoping that if their footsteps were later retraced by others, this too would throw pursuers off the scent. They then alighted at the next station — at Bromsgrove — which is but a short distance away from Nanny Jones's cottage at Elmbridge,' said Ravenscroft pausing for his words to take effect.

'How the devil do you know all this?' asked a crestfallen Sir Charles.

'Because before I came here this morning, I sought out Nanny Jones's cottage in Elmbridge. Whilst there I was able to complete my enquiries. Crabb, if you will please,' said Ravenscroft turning towards his constable.

All eyes turned in Crabb's direction, as he opened the door.

'Hello, Charles,' said a tall, gaunt, figure stepping into the room.

'Master Peter. You are alive!' exclaimed Jukes.

'Very much so. How are you, Jukes?' asked the man coming forwards and shaking the old butler's hand.

'Well sir, and all the better for seeing you, sir.'

'Charles, you have done me a grave injustice,' said Peter turning in his brother's direction, who in turn had covered his ashen face with his hands. 'A grave injustice indeed.'

'I . . . only acted . . .' muttered Chilton.

'Can you imagine what it was like, Charles? All those years, living from day to day, in a small room, seeing no one from the outside world, trying to explain to the authorities there that a gross injustice had been committed, knowing that the woman you loved had been stolen from you — and all that time waiting for that one day when someone would return to tell the truth, or I would be offered one opportunity to escape from that living hell. No, you have no comprehension of the wrong you have done me,' said an embittered Peter Chilton.

'But what about Old John? Who killed Old John?' asked Russell.

'John had seen Peter and Mildred in the churchyard that day. That was why he was afraid of the tomb, when Crabb and I encountered him there. "He's come back for me," the poor, deranged man cried, forgetting that his former master was not dead, and thinking that you, Master Peter, had risen from the dead and come back to claim him,' said Ravenscroft knowing that he was now arriving at the conclusion of his declaration.

'So you killed Old John,' said Sir Charles looking up at his brother.

'No, Sir Charles,' answered Ravenscroft, 'your brother was completely unaware that he had been seen by John when he and Mildred left the churchyard together; therefore had no reason to return there later to kill the old man.'

'Then who did?' asked Russell.

'Someone who was also there that day and had witnessed Old John crying out before the family tomb; someone who guessed that a familiar figure from the past had returned; someone who then knew that he had to silence the old man as soon as possible, before he told everything to me and my colleague; someone who was anxious to conceal the past as much as possible — and that someone was you, Sir Charles,' said Ravenscroft emphatically turning to face the master of Hill Court.

'Confound you, Ravenscroft!' snarled Chilton.

'Sir Charles Chilton, I am arresting you for the forcible abduction and imprisonment of your brother Peter Chilton, and for the murder of Old John. Crabb, put the cuffs on him,' instructed Ravenscroft.

Crabb marched over to Sir Charles and placed the brace-lets around his wrists.

'But where is Mildred?' asked Miss Petterson.

'Miss Chilton is alive and well. You will find her with Mrs Greenway in the kitchens,' said Ravenscroft walking over to the doors and opening them to reveal two uniformed officers standing in the hallway. 'Men, if you will accompany Sir Charles and Constable Crabb to the station, I will join you presently.'

'Peter . . . I am sorry . . . I meant no harm . . . can you forgive me,' muttered Sir Charles as he was about to be escorted from the room.

'I want nothing from you, brother, except one thing,' said Peter.

'What is that? Name it, and it will be yours,' replied Sir Charles looking anxiously into his brother's eyes.

'Sign this letter, authorizing the release of your wife Lady Mary,' said Peter taking a sheet of paper from the top pocket of his coat.

'Crabb, take Sir Charles to his desk, and remove the cuffs, so he is able to sign the authority,' instructed Ravenscroft.

Crabb escorted his prisoner back to his desk. A crest-fallen Sir Charles signed the paper and handed it to his brother. Crabb locked the cuffs once more around the salt baron's wrists.

'Well, Inspector, I cannot thank you enough. I suppose you will now be charging me with Mildred's abduction,' said Peter Chilton when the officers and their prisoner had left the room.

'Oh, I think that will not be necessary, sir. You have been through a great deal these past ten years. I think we all conclude that the girl went with you of her own free will,' replied Ravenscroft.

'Thank you, Inspector,' said Peter shaking the extended hand.

'Now, Miss Petterson, your charge awaits. I am sure she will be delighted to see you,' said Ravenscroft.

'Yes, of course,' replied the governess.

'What will you do now, Inspector?' asked Russell.

'Mr Chilton, if you would hand me the paper, and Mr Brockway if you would care to accompany my constable and me back to the asylum at Powick. There is a lady there, who has also been the victim of a grave injustice, who needs to be released, and to be reunited with her daughter,' smiled Ravenscroft.

EPILOGUE

'Miss Corbett must have been delighted when you returned her baby to her?' said Ravenscroft, as he and his wife sat together later that evening.

'Oh you should have seen the joy on her face, Samuel, as she held her Lily again in her arms,' smiled Lucy.

'Let us hope that she is not compelled to sell her baby to the next old woman who comes along, offering to raise the child as her own for a few guineas.'

'I am sure she will not. I think the farmer at Wellington Heath has agreed that the child can stay, and I have told Miss Corbett that if she ever finds herself in difficulties in the future she is to have no hesitation in calling upon us for our assistance. I hope you do not mind?'

'Of course not, my dear,' said Samuel taking his wife's hand. 'I would have expected nothing less from your generous nature. What about the boy? I think you said his name was Harold.'

'He has been taken to the workhouse in Kidderminster. It seems that his mother was compelled to hand him over to that terrible woman some months ago before sailing for a new life in Australia. It will be difficult to trace her.'

'The poor child, whatever will become of him? The workhouse is no place for a destitute boy of his age.'

'Mr Shorter has told me that it his intention to apply to the workhouse authorities to have the boy apprenticed at his newspaper office.'

'That is good news indeed. It is pleasing to know that some good will come out of all this. It is a pity however that that evil Drew woman managed to elude the authorities. I will contact all the local stations and ask them to keep a sharp look out for her. She cannot hide from us forever,' said Ravenscroft.

'I wonder what makes such a woman take on unwanted children in such a fashion?'

'Greed, my dear. I have heard of one or two similar stories over the years, where poor unfortunate women have given their children away for a few coins, believing that their offspring will be given a new life full of opportunities. In fact the opposite is often the case. The baby farmers — for that is I believe what these horrible wretches are called — are only interested in receiving the money. They have no interest in the children who are placed in their care. The poor unfortunate child is often never heard of again, and one can only suppose that he or she is either left to die through neglect and want, or is killed in a brutal fashion by their supposed benefactors.'

'It is fortunate that the horrible woman had not killed poor Lily before we were able to rescue her.'

'I can only consider that her interest in keeping the child alive for so long, was because she hoped she might be able to sell her on to some childless couple. When she knew that we were closing in on her, she then sought to rid herself of the child in the canal.'

'It is a horrible business,' said Lucy recoiling.

'I have no doubt that the evil Huddlestone/Drew woman will be arrested soon, and that she will then be made to account for her crimes before a judge and jury.'

'Let us hope so. Women like that are a wicked presence in society. How clever you were to find Mildred Chilton.'

'She seems none the worse for her ordeal. Nanny Jones and Peter took good care of her. I think she rather enjoyed the experience.'

'And thank goodness that you were able to rescue poor Lady Chilton from that horrible asylum place.'

'Her wretched husband had treated her in such a brutal manner, and had enlisted the assistance of Doctor Staples in having her put away inside the asylum. The man was like those characters you have been reading about in Mr Stevenson's novel; outwardly Sir Charles acted the part of a professional businessman and landed gentleman, whilst in truth, he was a ruthless villain who would stop at nothing to obtain what he wanted.'

'It is Peter Chilton whom I feel sorry for. It must have been awful to be incarcerated in that place for ten years, against his will, with no one there to believe in his pro-testations,' said Lucy. 'I suppose when he finally escaped he sought revenge by taking Mildred away from her parents. Do you think he believed that Mildred was his own daughter?'

'I think that was probably the case. Anyway, no harm has come to the girl and she is now reunited with her mother.'

'What I don't understand is if Sir Charles wanted to get rid of his brother all those years ago, why did he not kill him and put him in the coffin, rather than imprisoning him in the asylum?' asked Lucy.

'I suppose he could not bring himself to commit such a final atrocity. He was family after all. He must have had some feeling for his brother.'

'What will happen to him now?'

'He will stand trial for the murder of Old John, and for the false imprisonment of his brother.'

'So Peter will come into his inheritance again?' asked Lucy.

'Indeed.'

'You were very clever in realizing where Peter and Mildred were.'

'It was Mrs Greenway, the cook, who provided the solution, although I did not see it as such at the time. It was only when I remembered Old John's words in the churchyard, that it all made sense. For a while I had thought that your Mrs Drew had taken Mildred, but of course there was no connection between the two cases.'

'Samuel, now that both our cases of missing children have come to a satisfactory conclusion,. perhaps you might find the time to go and visit that house in Malvern that I was telling you about,' said Lucy smiling at her husband.

'Of course my dear. You are quite right. This place is far too small for us all. We shall go shortly. However, there is just one more thing that I need to do tomorrow . . .'

* * *

Ravenscroft stood at the side of the open grave in Dodderhill as the two men lowered the plain simple coffin into the ground. He brushed the rain from his wind-swept face and remembered the days of his own lonely childhood, as the clergyman spoke the last words of the ceremony.

'Would you care to say a few words, Mr Ravenscroft?'

Ravenscroft paused for a moment, wondering whether he should say some words of final farewell, but then realizing that he was unable to do so, he merely shook his head from side to side.

The gravedigger reached for his spade.

'One moment,' interjected Ravenscroft reaching into the pocket of his overcoat and taking out a small packet. 'I should like this . . .'

The words seemed to die before he had spoken them.

'Of course,' said the clergyman. 'You appear to be the only person here today to say farewell to her, Mr Ravenscroft?'

'Yes.'

'She must have been alone in the world?'

'Yes.'

'No relatives other than yourself?'

'No. I am — I never knew her.'

'I see. May I ask—' began the clergyman.

'I did not want her to be alone,' replied Ravenscroft kneeling at the side of the grave and throwing the packet onto the top of the coffin. 'She did not deserve to die alone in that house in Worcester. She did not deserve that. I did not want her to be alone.'

'Very noble and Christian of you, sir, if I may say so. Very noble indeed.'

Ravenscroft turned away from the scene.

'Mr Ravenscroft just before you go, I wonder what name you would like engraved on the stone?'

Ravenscroft hesitated.

'Of course if you prefer, my dear sir, we could leave the stone unmarked.'

'No I would not like that. She must have a name. Anne,' said Ravenscroft suddenly. 'I should like the name Anne to be engraved on the stone. Anne with an "e". if you will be so kind.'

'Will that be all, sir?'

'Yes — just Anne, if you would.'

* * *

As Ravenscroft left the churchyard the black clouds parted and a ray of sunshine shone down on the wet path. Closing the gate behind him he began to make his way down the winding lane. Gradually he saw a group of three familiar figures in the distance, coming forwards to meet him.

'Mr Ravenscroft, we could not let you leave without saying goodbye,' said Lady Chilton greeting him encouragingly.

'That is most kind. I trust you are now fully recovered from your ordeal, Lady Chilton?'

'My doctors expect me to make a full recovery,' smiled the lady.

194

'That is good, and how are you, Miss Mildred?' asked Ravenscroft turning his attention towards the young girl who clasped her mother's hand.

'I am well, sir, thank you,' replied the girl.

'Mr Chilton,' said Ravenscroft shaking Peter's hand.

'Ravenscroft, we cannot thank you enough.'

'Take good care of Lady Chilton and her daughter, they have been through a great deal,' said Ravenscroft.

'I intend to,' smiled Chilton.

'Have you heard the news, Mr Ravenscroft?' said Lady Chilton. 'Miss Petterson and Mr Russell are to be married.'

'That is good news indeed. You will be in need of a new governess then, Miss Chilton?' suggested Ravenscroft.

'Miss Petterson has agreed that she will continue to look after Mildred after she is married,' replied Lady Chilton.

'Then all ends well. I trust that you will all be able to put the past behind you. I wish you all good day,' said Ravenscroft raising his hat.

'Good morning to you, Inspector.'

The couple, holding the hands of the small girl, watched, as the detective made his way down the lane — and out of sight.

POSTSCRIPT

Sir Charles Chilton was found guilty of the murder of Old John, and of the false incarceration of his brother Peter, and was hanged at Worcester Gaol.

Peter Chilton came into his inheritance once more and married his former betrothed. They had two children and lived for many years at Hill Court. The property was later sold and became a successful private school.

* * *

On 30th March, 1896, a bargeman on the River Thames at Reading recovered a brown paper parcel from the murky waters of the nearby canal. The parcel contained the body of an infant girl, and an examination of the deceased showed that she had been strangled with some layers of tape. Lettering on the outside of the brown paper parcel, however, revealed the name of a Mrs Thomas of Piggott's Road, Lower Caversham.

Police enquiries later identified Mrs Thomas to be one Amelia Elizabeth Dyer. The river and canal were dragged for other bodies, and the decomposed corpses of two baby boys were recovered from the waters. Four other bodies of young children were found later.

Amelia Dyer stood trial for her crimes at the Old Bailey in London, where a jury took just five minutes to find her guilty. She was hanged at Newgate prison on 10th June, 1896.

Although it is known that Amelia Dyer killed at least seven children, it is generally assumed that she had killed many.

THE END

ALSO BY KERRY TOMBS

**INSPECTOR RAVENSCROFT
DETECTIVE MYSTERIES**

Book 1: THE MALVERN MURDERS
Book 2: THE WORCESTER WHISPERERS
Book 3: THE LEDBURY LAMPLIGHTERS Book
4: THE TEWKESBURY TOMB
Book 5: THE DROITWICH DECEIVERS

Please join our mailing list for free Kindle historical
fiction, sagas, romance books, mysteries and crime
thrillers, and new releases!

www.joffebooks.com

FREE KINDLE BOOKS

Printed in Great Britain
by Amazon